She twisted away from him in alarm

"Stay away from me, Joss," Meredith warned. He towered over her, and she was more sexually aware of him than she had been of any man. He took hold of her, his hands caressed her back and ecstasy flowed through her. For a few moments she abandoned herself to it, but when his hand slipped around to touch her breast, she was awakened to the madness in which they were indulging, and she dragged herself away from him.

"I don't want you near me!" she gasped.

"You could have fooled me," he drawled. "If that's the way you reacted to Piers Loring he was a very lucky guy."

"Piers would never have taken advantage of a situation like this. You had no business touching me. I hated it! I don't want you near me again!" she cried, regardless of whether it was the truth.

"We'll see." Joss smiled.

PAMELA POPE

eden's law

Harlequin Books

TORONTO · NEW YORK · LONDON
AMSTERDAM · PARIS · SYDNEY · HAMBURG
STOCKHOLM · ATHENS · TOKYO · MILAN

Harlequin Presents first edition September 1983
ISBN 0-373-10628-9

Original hardcover edition published in 1983
by Mills & Boon Limited

CHAPTER ONE

MEREDITH was not in the best of moods when she pushed open the door of the New Inn and went inside. Her feet hurt from walking nearly a mile downhill in high-heeled sandals, and the case she hadn't liked to leave in an unattended car felt as if it was dislocating her shoulder. So it didn't improve matters when she heard the landlord too engrossed in conversation with someone in the other bar to pay any attention.

It was not until she realised they were talking about *her* that she listened unashamedly, and she tensed with indignation.

'They tell me the Paxton girl's coming back here to live,' she heard the landlord say. 'How does that grab you?'

'It doesn't,' said another male voice. 'Secretary, and more, to a self-made millionaire who got himself killed in his private plane! Sad they both ran out of luck.' His tone was disparaging, completely lacking in sympathy.

The landlord laughed. 'The newspapers made a meal of it. But I suppose you had inside information.'

'None. The Paxtons are fine people. I only hope their spoilt only daughter will appreciate the fatted calf.'

Her eyes were smarting at the unwarranted attack and anger was a stabbing pain. How dared two total strangers talk about her like that, as if she had committed a sin! What right had they to pass judgment on someone they had never met? It was the two little words 'and more' that really infuriated her, implying a wealth of meaning for which there was no justification. It was unfair, unforgivable!

She put the case down out of the way and went

5

through to the other bar, her back straight as a rod, chin held high and the light of battle in her eyes. The landlord had measured a tot of whisky into a glass and was splashing soda into it before passing it to his customer, but he paused when Meredith tapped on the bar with long, immaculate fingernails.

'Please can you tell me where there's a phone I can use,' she said. 'My car's broken down and I want to get home. I take it there's a public telephone here?'

'There is indeed. Through the door and into the passage. It's in a recess on the left.'

'Thank you.' She inclined her head in acknowledgement. 'By the way, my name is Meredith Paxton.'

The landlord shifted his glasses down to the tip of his nose and peered at her over the top of them, frowning. The other man lifted his head, fixing her with a strange, almost cynical look. A shaft of early evening sunlight found its way through the mullioned window and settled on him. His eyes were the colour of green olives, and the intensity of his gaze disconcerted her, in spite of having the advantage. She was not oblivious to the attraction of craggy features and thick brown hair which feathered straight across his forehead, long enough to tip on the collar of his navy-blue shirt at the back. The suggestion of a smile touched his mouth, but neither he nor the landlord offered an apology for their comments which they must have known she had heard. Not liking the way he scrutinised her, she flicked her head to break the unwanted contact and walked past him disdainfully.

The inn had a warm, malty smell and drowsed in a country quietness. It was going to be difficult to come to terms with the quietness again after city life, but in a way she welcomed it. Or she had done until a few minutes ago. She had loved London, but without Piers there was nothing to stay for and she had thought it would be easier living where she was not continually reminded of things they had done together. But she hadn't been prepared for vindictiveness as soon as she set foot in Edencombe, and she didn't understand it, because surely a family feud was nothing to do with outsiders.

She found five pence for the phone and lifted the receiver, but made no effort to dial the number. Her desire for haste had evaporated. She had chosen to come home via the deserted top road that led down from the moors so that she could stop at the highest point and view the village from a distance first, afraid of being drawn back into the old ways before she was ready. She'd been looking forward to coming home, but she still had reservations. She wouldn't be able to talk about Piers, for one thing, but being reconciled with her parents after two long years was some recompence, and she prayed the feud would now be forgotten.

She dialled the number slowly and waited, half turning so that she caught sight of her reflection in an oval mirror on the opposite wall. The soft light showed up shadows beneath her hazel eyes. Glossy dark hair fell smoothly from a centre parting that started from a perfect widow's peak and was coiled elegantly at the crown of her head, giving her poise, but the radiance that had added so much to an intriguing beauty was no longer in evidence.

'Combe Lodge. Mrs Paxton speaking.'

Meredith was surprised to hear her mother's voice and she fumbled with the money which had been balanced ready to insert for several seconds.

'Mummy, it's me. I'm at the New Inn.'

'Meredith darling!' her mother exclaimed. 'I'm so relieved to hear you, but what on earth are you doing there?'

'Something's wrong with my car,' said Meredith, the

warmth of her mother's welcome washing over her like a soothing balm. 'Please will you ask Daddy to come and fetch me.'

'Your father's out, I'm afraid. He went after lunch and I don't know what time he'll be back. And my car is in the garage for servicing, so can you get a taxi? I can do with you here, darling. I'm up to my eyes in jam making for a Sale of Work tomorrow.'

Meredith smiled. Nothing had changed. It was just as if she was still coming home every weekend, being confronted by her mother's never-ending charitable jobs with which she always needed help. She'd never thought she would be pleased to hear the familiar cry, but at that moment it almost brought a lump to her throat. No need to worry whether she was going to be made welcome.

'I'll make it as soon as I can,' she promised.

She put the receiver back and searched her purse for another five pence, but she was right out of change and she clicked her tongue with annoyance. Brandishing a pound note, she returned to the bar, hoping the man with green eyes would have left, but he was still there, his back towards her.

'I'm afraid my father's out and I've got to phone for a taxi,' she said. 'Can you split this for me, please?'

'No problem,' said the landlord, taking the note over to the till. 'You've had a bit of a rough time, Miss Paxton.'

'Yes,' she said. His tone, at least, was now sympathetic and he was trying to make amends without actually apologising. He handed her the change, obviously uncomfortable because he couldn't look at her squarely, and she didn't help him by making any comment. The local paper had probably gone to town on the story anyway.

She turned to go back to the phone, glad she had

learned not to show her feelings. By ignoring their slander while at the same time letting them know she was aware of it had strengthened her position, and their discomfort made her smile inwardly. But then the other man stood up, barring her way, and she saw that he was not the slightest bit abashed.

'Perhaps I can give you a lift to the village,' he said.

He was quite a giant and the oak beams came perilously near to the top of his head. His voice was as warm and smooth as dark sherry, and like sherry it went straight to her bloodstream, affecting her legs with a weakness that spread down to her toes. She hadn't noticed it until he towered over her.

She refused the offer on principle. 'Thank you, but I prefer to get a taxi.' He needn't think she could be placated so easily, and she hadn't really been taken in by the voice. The peculiar trembling in her legs was only to be expected after staggering downhill on precarious heels and wouldn't have occurred if she had worn flat shoes.

The landlord closed the till and looked at the tall man, straight-faced.

'She doesn't trust you, Joss.'

'She doesn't like me, Sid. Can't say I blame her.' He slapped the bar with the palm of his hand before departing. 'Cheers. I'll be in touch.'

Meredith went back to the phone and dialled the taxi number given on a printed card above the coinbox, but with no success. There had been a wedding in the village and the only local taxi was engaged elsewhere, so she was faced with a long walk home. If only she had used the low road to Edencombe like everyone else none of this would have happened. Too late to reconsider her refusal of a lift even if she wanted to, and she didn't really regret it anyway. She'd hated the way the man had stared at her, and she had seen that expression too often not to recognise it. Those green eyes had studied her with expertise, giving her the once-over quite blatantly. No doubt soft-tongued flattery also came easily with a voice like that, and she wouldn't have wanted to give him the chance to practise any.

She went back to the bar, tired, lonely and dispirited. She wished she had packed a more comfortable pair of shoes, but she would not be beaten.

'Seems like I'll have to walk after all,' she said, as she went to lift her case.

'Would you like to leave that case here and have someone pick it up later?' the landlord asked.

'Thanks, but I'd rather take it with me,' she said quickly. It weighed a ton, but it contained the essentials she would need before her trunks arrived, and there was her jewel case inside with a valuable collection of presents Piers had bought her.

'Please yourself.' He turned away, but not before she had seen an aggravating smirk on his lips. 'You should have gone with Joss. He might have introduced himself properly.'

Not bothering to ask what he meant by that odd remark, she left the inn and set off again in the city sandals, hoping she wouldn't get too many blisters.

The sun was low, lending a toffee-coloured glow to everything, and it was still warm. The inn stood alone on a high stretch of road that lay open to all weathers, and some distance below was the North Devon village of Edencombe, a haze of mist tendrils gathering between the chimneys. It was still called a village, though lately it had grown so much in size it had become a small town. To the left was the church, its spire peering above the trees as if on tiptoe, and the original houses clustered round it haphazardly. Among them was Combe Lodge, and to take her mind off her feet Meredith traced the road to it, her eyes travelling westward until she could just make out the firs and tall chimneys. It looked as far away as ever, and she felt as if it was Piers still holding her back by an invisible thread, despising her for accepting the olive branch which she had longed to be offered when he was alive.

She would never forget her parents' reaction when she told them she had met Piers Loring and agreed to put money into a business project he intended starting. They were horrified, incredulous, and convinced they could talk her out of it.

'He's the son of MacDonald Loring,' her father had said, in strident tones, as if that was sufficient condemnation. When she didn't answer he went on, 'The man's gone bankrupt twice. The first time he was going to marry your mother and he took all her money to pay off his debts, then he cleared off and left her.'

'I know all about Mac Loring. I've heard about him ever since I was old enough to understand,' said Meredith. 'It's not him I'm investing money with, and you've got to believe that Piers isn't like him. He has this great idea for making young fashions on a budget, and I don't think it can fail, so I'm prepared to back him. It's my money and I'm twenty-one, so you can't persuade me otherwise.'

'But, Meredith, your law studies . . .' her mother protested.

'I'm giving them up. I'm going to be Piers's secretary.'

She remembered how the row had escalated, everyone saying cruel things which couldn't be recalled, but she was adamant. She had met Piers at university and he had been confident enough in his own ability to risk dropping his studies, so Meredith had felt justified in giving up hers.

'And when I've made enough money I'll be able to pay you back what Mac Loring owes you, then perhaps this vendetta can be forgotten,' she had said to her mother.

'I wouldn't touch a penny of it,' said Julia Paxton. 'Tainted money, that's what it would be. Anything to do with that family is rotten.'

'I'll prove you wrong,' said Meredith. 'Next time I come home I'll bring Piers with me.'

'If you throw in your lot with the Lorings, Meredith, you won't be welcome in this house again,' her father had warned, 'so there's no question of your bringing *him* here to upset your mother.'

Meredith's chin had lifted defiantly. 'That's all right. I'll take all my things with me and find a flat in London. I'm not a child, and you can't arrange *my* life to suit you.'

Her mother had then tried to become a mediator, heartbroken at the turn of events and desperate to avoid losing her daughter, but Meredith had inherited her father's unyielding spirit and there was no way anyone could get round her. The cloud under which she had left Edencombe hadn't lifted until the news of Piers's death brought the first overture of reconciliation from her parents. Piers would have been ashamed of her for being weak enough to accept it, but without him it was pointless to deny herself the love of parents who had never ceased to be infinitely dear to her, and had agreed to wipe the slate clean and start again.

The bottle-green skirt stopped swirling as she walked down the hill, clinging to her legs as she got hotter. The thin leather straps across her toes pinched harder and every step hurt a little more. She began counting the steps and each time she got to fifty she changed the case over to the other hand, but it was getting heavier all the time and her palms felt raw. It was just as she was making the fourth transfer that the weight seemed to take over and the case swung outwards of its own volition, pulling her off balance. She fell with an undignified thump, one foot doubled under her, and the case slithered away across the warm tarmac just as a car was coming up from the village. The front wheel touched it, sent it skidding further, and the impact was too much for the already over-strained catches, making them burst open. To her horror Meredith saw her belongings scattered all over the road.

She yelled and tried to get to her feet, but a scalding pain shot through her ankle, enough to bring tears to her eyes, and she was helpless. The car pulled up, then reversed until it was level with her, and the driver got out, a murderous look on his face. It was the man called Joss.

'You're damned lucky you didn't cause a serious accident!' he bellowed. 'What on earth do you think you're doing in the middle of the road?'

'Well, I'm not waiting for a bus!' she retaliated. Couldn't the idiot see she had fallen? She made another attempt to stand, but got no further than her knees. She glared at him. 'Nor am I praying for deliverance, so you needn't stand there like an avenging angel! Oh, no! My best silk nightie!'

A van coming down the hill had swerved to avoid them and ploughed through an assortment of costly underwear, leaving tyre marks. Joss surveyed the scene with scorn, but when Meredith sank back with a gasp after trying again to put her weight on her foot he leaned towards her.

'Do you wish me to handle your intimate possessions, or wait until I've handled *you* first? You obviously need help.'

He went behind her, put his hands beneath her arms and helped her up with ease, but the foot was already swelling and turning a nasty colour and she couldn't put it to the ground. Her face went white. If he hadn't been supporting her she would have fallen.

'I was due at a meeting at seven, but it looks as if I'll

have to be late,' he said. 'If you hadn't been so pigheaded in the first place you could have been home by now all in one piece.'

Without any more preamble he slipped a hand beneath her knees and swung her into his arms, carrying her across the road to his car. Every nerve in her body became tense, fighting against contact with him, but she was entirely dependent on his help, so it was no use protesting, even when a peculiar panic assailed her.

'I'm sorry I've got to take up some of your time and petrol,' she said when he set her down and opened the car door. 'I'm quite willing to pay. . . . Ow!'

Her wrist was caught in a vice-like grip. 'If you ever offer me money again, Miss Paxton, you'll regret it!'

'If you're trying to incapacitate me altogether, you're succeeding. Let me go!'

They glowered at each other, igniting sparks with every word, and when he did as she asked she fell back on to the car seat with a gasp. What force was this she had come up against?

She watched him go to retrieve her things. Another car drove over them and she held her breath when it just missed the suede jewellery box. Joss picked up the case and began ramming things into it without any care, and she didn't take her eyes off him until her jewels were safely stowed away. Before leaving London she had packed everything meticulously, but now, with nothing folded, the case was too full to close and the only way he could fasten it was by sitting on the lid. Meredith pressed her fingers to her temples in despair, shuddering when he finally dropped the case into the trunk.

'You might as well have packed the wardrobe as well,' he said.

He slid one long leg over the driving seat and levered himself into the car. Piers had always sat down first and swung his legs round with one lithe movement in keeping with his slim figure. Funny, she had never realised before that even the simple action of getting into a car could differ noticeably from one person to another.

The road was not wide enough to do a U-turn and Joss had to drive up to the New Inn again before he could turn round and head back to the village.

'Tell me, what made you come back to Edencombe?' he asked. 'Surely the Piers Loring Group won't fold without its founder. I would have thought you'd prefer to stay on.'

Meredith glanced at his aristocratic profile, dismayed at the anger his patronising tone aroused. He spoke of Piers as if he had started a little tin-pot corner shop instead of a clothing industry with outlets in every part of the world, and she longed to wipe that supercillious expression off his face.

'There are several reasons why I chose not to, none of which are anything to do with you,' she said. 'In fact I find your comments about my affairs altogether distasteful.'

He ignored the censure. 'You didn't fancy a new boss in the same firm, then.'

'No, I didn't.'

Her lack of encouragement made conversation difficult, but after a moment's thought, he said: 'You're probably right. If you were one person's exclusive property, indoctrinated with his ideas, it would be difficult to make adjustments.'

It was as if he disapproved of her and was trying to cut her down. She didn't understand it, and strongly objected, but what point was there in starting an argument with an impertinent bystander? In the last two months she had built a protective wall around herself to keep the curious at bay and she was certainly

not going to let this ignorant stranger knock holes in it.
Her ankle throbbed, adding physical pain to the burden
of her resentment, and she diverted the subject into a
safer channel.

'Edencombe is my home and I've always loved it,' she
said. 'My father is a solicitor here, as I'm sure you
know, and he's taken on a new partner who will be
needing a secretary, so it seemed like a good idea for me
to take on the job.'

'And how does the new partner feel about having the
power behind a tycoon thrust upon him?'

She smiled for the first time. 'He's an old chap called
Joseph Hamblyn,' she said, 'and if he's got any sense
he'll count his blessings. In case you're in any doubt, I
happen to be a very good secretary. I. . . . Hey, where
are you taking me?'

The cry came as he suddenly turned left into a gravel
drive that led to one of the loveliest houses in
Edencombe. It was an old white farmhouse, irregular in
shape, its red-tiled roof sweeping almost to the ground
at one end, windows stacking to two stories at the other
where the lawn sloped down to a pond edged with trees.
As long as she could remember Meredith had admired
the house and wondered what it was like inside. It was
called Eden Farm.

'I live here,' said Joss. He looked at his watch. 'It's
too late for the doctor's surgery, and as Ellen was a
nurse I'll get her to see what damage you've done to
that ankle. If she thinks you've broken anything I'll
have to take you over to Casualty.'

'You really don't have to bother,' she protested.

'I know I don't,' he said. 'I'm afraid the house is
in chaos. It's Kirsty's birthday and she's having a
party.'

He drew up outside a white front door with a
wrought iron lamp hanging above it, and when he

switched off the engine she could hear childish shrieks coming from the garden. Never having had much to do with children she was rather in awe of them, and she hoped they were better mannered than their father.

He got out of the car and came round to open her door. When he helped her up she winced with the movement and almost overbalanced as she tottered on one high heel. He grabbed her arm.

'For Pete's sake take those ridiculous shoes off!' he snapped. 'If you'd had sense enough to walk barefoot you wouldn't have hurt yourself. Pride certainly came before *that* fall.'

'Don't be so damned smart!'

She sat back on the seat, quivering with anger. What an abominable man he was! He didn't deserve to live in this idyllic house, and she was already sorry for his wife and family. Was he always so overbearing? She longed to stalk away and have nothing more to do with him, and she was on the point of asking him to take her straight on to Combe Lodge when the front door opened and a young woman came out. She had short brown hair, cut elfin fashion so that it needed little attention, and was of medium height. There were flip-flops on her feet and her dress was of faded cotton, but her smile was the loveliest thing Meredith had seen for a long time.

'Joss, I thought you were at your meeting by now,' she called.

'Can you phone and tell them I'll be late. And then can you have a look at Miss Paxton's ankle, Ellen, and see what she's done to it.'

Meredith felt embarrassed. He didn't even know how to say please, but as he helped her out of the car the girl came forward, her eyes lighting up with pleasure.

'Why, Miss Paxton, how nice you two have met! I'm Ellen Munro. Joss'll take you in while I just make a

phone call for him. Looks like you've got a bad sprain
there. I'll find some strapping for it. Joss, be careful. Do
you want me to come round the other side?'

'I'm so sorry to be such a nuisance,' said Meredith,
taking to the other girl immediately. Her friendliness
was overwhelming, and made up for her boorish
husband. 'I can manage perfectly, and I really ought to
get home as soon as possible.'

'But not until I've had a look at that sprain. Joss did
right to bring you here first.'

She dashed off indoors. Meredith clung to Joss's arm
while she removed the offending sandals, then hobbled
painfully into the house with him, trying not to show
how much her ankle hurt in case he was tempted to
pick her up again. The thought of him doing so filled
her with dread.

The house was as lovely inside as it was out, and she
was spellbound. It wasn't luxuriously furnished, but as
soon as she entered the hall she was aware of a happy
atmosphere and had the ridiculous notion that she only
had to stay here and her troubles would be washed
away. The mellow golden walls seemed to fold her in
comforting stillness and the tick of the grandfather
clock eased her heartbeats to a similar rhythm, gentle
and soothing.

'This is beautiful,' she breathed, and for a moment
even the supporting arm of the man beside her was not
alien.

He looked at her keenly. 'I'm glad you like it. We'll
go through to the kitchen.'

The spell was broken. He helped her down the hall,
past a lounge where Ellen was using the phone, and
Meredith saw chairs covered with rust-brown chintz.
The kitchen floor had rush matting over dark red
quarry tiles and there were copper pans and baskets
hanging from hooks in the ceiling, just as they would

have been when this was a working farm. Joss deposited her on an antique settle, and her ribs felt bruised where his fingers had dug into her.

'Stay there,' he said. 'I'll send Ellen out to you. Sounds like I'd better speak to the man myself.'

She apologised again, 'I really am sorry. . . .' But he had gone, and she didn't know whether he had heard.

She looked around with interest, deciding to ignore his brusqueness. An Aga stove filled one corner and a kettle was boiling away on it merrily. Every surface was covered with the remnants of a party—empty plastic beakers with bent straws, ice cream dishes, squashed fruit and paper serviettes crushed and torn beyond recognition, and there were toys everywhere. A baby was asleep in a carry-cot on the pinewood table. The back door stood open and as Ellen returned a horde of children surged in from the garden, shouting, laughing, crying. The noise was deafening.

'Mummy, Mummy, I can't find my teddy bear. Shaun took it and I want it. Make him give it to me!' cried a little girl. Her short brown hair and round eyes were so much like Ellen's that it would have been impossible to mistake her for anyone else's child.

'I didn't take it,' protested a small boy of about five. 'Gary's hidden it because we're playing hunt the bear.'

'Well, can't you hunt something else?' said Ellen— 'I don't think Teddy will like being hidden away on his own, do you? How would *you* like it, Gary? Give it back to Kirsty.'

The second boy was perhaps two years older, with short cropped hair and a tough little face which somehow seemed out of place here. If he was a party guest Meredith wondered why he had been invited.

'I wouldn't care. I've often been locked in a cupboard,' he said, shuffling his feet. 'Anyway, it's a stupid old bear.' He flung it at Kirsty who started to howl, and a storm broke loose as a dozen infant voices were raised. The baby in the carry-cot began to yell.

'That's enough!' Joss came back and stood in the doorway, his heavy brows lowered, a forbidding scowl darkening his face. His hands were on his hips. 'Outside, all of you! *Out!*' he roared. 'Gary, don't take Kirsty's teddy bear again!'

There was instant silence as every child turned to him. Meredith was horrified, sure he had scared them all to death. But Kirsty giggled, and the giggle spread like measles, infecting them all with squeals of laughter as they ran back to the garden.

A moment later Kirsty was back. 'Come outside and play with us,' she begged, tugging at Joss's hand. 'Please!'

'You horrible child,' said Joss, but the first faint smile touched his mouth. He set her aside and whacked her bottom, but instead of crying as Meredith expected, she creased into helpless laughter and ran off, followed by Joss, who picked up the screaming baby on his way and took him with him.

To Meredith, who was not used to family life, the scene was incredible. She was bewildered by the noise and assortment of children, and the way he had shouted at them. It didn't seem at all the way he should have spoken to them, yet they all seemed to find it great fun, and she had to presume his bark was worse than his bite. She had heard that children knew instinctively the people who liked them, but this man certainly had a very strange way of showing it. She was beginning to dislike him more every minute.

The quietness that followed was like the aftermath of a whirlwind. Ellen, unperturbed by it all, had filled a bowl with cold water and was smiling as she came over with it.

'Sorry about that,' she said. 'I don't know how Joss puts up with them. He's marvellous with children, he really is.'

Marvellous! That was not the word Meredith would have used.

'How many are yours?' she ventured to ask.

'Only two,' said Ellen. 'Kirsty and the baby, but I'm fostering Shaun and Gary for a while. The poor little things have come from rough homes and need a lot of love. Various parents will soon be coming for the others. It's been quite a day.'

Quite a day, Meredith echoed silently. What on earth had made this girl take on two extra children when she already had so much to cope with?

Ellen explored the ankle with expert fingers, declared there was nothing broken and applied cold compresses to ease the pain, and when she looked up at Meredith there was a certain tranquillity in her face which was inexplicable. Here she was, tied to the house by her family and impossible husband, yet she looked as happy as if she had all the riches in the world. To Meredith it would have seemed like a prison.

Ellen chatted on about the children as she wound a crêpe bandage round the swollen foot. Her face was animated, and Meredith glanced away. It was then she saw Joss in the garden with the baby resting on his shoulder, chin against the small fluffy head as he pacified it, and without warning a lump came into her throat. She had stumbled on something that defied explanation, and she understood Ellen a little better.

'I'm very grateful,' she said to her, when she hobbled out to the car again a short time later. The ankle was firmly strapped and a lot less painful. Parents were arriving, but Ellen Munro had come out with her while Joss rounded up straying children.

'I've really looked forward to meeting you,' said

Ellen. 'I know your mother very well and I'm very fond of her. Perhaps we can get to know each other better when the children aren't around.' She gave a yell as Kirsty launched herself at her skirt, then she put her hand to her mouth. 'I don't know whatever you must think of me! I've been babbling on about the children and haven't even enquired about you, Meredith, or asked how you are. I meant to have said how sorry I was. You don't mind me calling you Meredith, do you?'

Meredith smiled, almost tempted to put her arms round the other girl. She was the most warmhearted person she had met in a long while.

'I don't mind at all,' she said. 'And I'd much rather talk about you than me.'

Joss came striding over. 'Leave your mother alone!' he shouted to Kirsty. 'Go and help the boys to tidy the kitchen.'

'No!' cried Kirsty, her impish face daring him to touch her. She squirmed noisily as he pretended to give chase, then ran off indoors.

Ellen had been watching Meredith's expression, and she laughed. 'Don't let Joss upset you,' she said. 'It's just an act he puts on. He's a real softy underneath.'

Meredith found that very hard to believe. When she was sitting beside him in the car a few minutes later as he drove once more towards the village, she didn't know what to say, and an uneasy silence lengthened between them. She wanted to thank him, to comment on his house, tell him how much she liked Ellen, but words wouldn't come. His face in profile was stern, offering no friendly opening, and she was left in no doubt he still considered her a nuisance for making him miss his meeting.

They were turning into the entrance to Combe Lodge when he spoke.

'I phoned your mother and told her where you were. She would have been worrying.'

Meredith's eyes showed her surprise. 'That was kind of you. Thank you.'

'I didn't expect you to think of it,' he said, his tone derogatory. 'Thoughtfulness takes practice, and I hardly think you've had much of that.'

She was jolted out of her complacency. The words stung, as if he had handed her a bunch of stinging nettles, and she wanted to cry out against the injustice. Tears pricked the back of her eyes, but one thing she never did was weep, and she was not going to let this objectionable man speak to her like that and get away with it.

'I don't know what's the matter with you,' she said icily. 'You don't even know me, and I've done nothing to deserve the rudeness you've dished out ever since we met. I refuse to take any more of it. Thank you for your begrudging help, and I hope our paths never cross again.'

There, that would show him!

She waited for another outburst in reply, and when none came she thought she had scored, until he suddenly chuckled. She could hardly believe her ears when such a pleasantly human sound came from him. She looked up sharply, wondering what he found funny, but there was no time to ask because they were at the door, and her mother was there.

'Meredith darling, what an awful thing to happen as soon as you get home! What a good job Joss was there. Can you manage to walk?'

She ran towards her as Meredith opened the car door, rubbing sticky hands in her apron, and a moment later they were enveloped in each other's arms.

'Oh, Mummy, I'm *so* glad to see you!'

Joss was taking her case from the trunk and he carried

it inside the house as if he was used to going in and out of the place. Julia Paxton turned to him.

'Thank you so much, Joss. Whatever would we do without you!'

'It was a pleasure,' said Joss. The engine was still running and he got back in the car. It moved slowly away. 'Tell Howard I'll try and make the last part of the meeting.'

'Don't worry about it, my dear. I'm sure Howard won't. Our daughter is more important.'

Meredith faced her mother. 'How do you come to know Joss Munro so well?' she asked, with a trembling inside her that was akin to hostility. Surely her mother didn't like the wretched man.

'Munro?' said Mrs Paxton, with a puzzled shake of her head. 'That's Joss Hamblyn, darling, your father's new partner. Ellen Munro is his sister.'

CHAPTER TWO

HOWARD PAXTON roared with laughter when he heard about the trick Joss had played.

'That's just typical,' he said. 'Joss always enjoys a good joke.'

'Well, *I* didn't find it funny,' snapped Meredith. 'I think he'd made up his mind to dislike me even before we met and he did nothing but antagonise me. I'm sorry, Daddy, but I find your Mr Hamblyn quite impossible.'

They had just finished dinner. It had been a very happy occasion, almost like old times, and if she had had any doubts about the wisdom of returning home they were all dispelled. Her parents had gone out of their way to make her feel wanted. Even the meal had been her favourite steak and kidney pie, which no one could bake quite so deliciously as her mother. The only thing which caused slight tension was the deliberate evasion of any reference to Piers, and there was danger of the omission growing in importance, but she hadn't the courage yet to touch on the subject.

And until now there had been no mention of Joss Hamblyn, for which she was thankful. No way could she find anything pleasant to say about him, and she would have hated to start off the evening on a sour note. Then her mother related the saga of the mistaken identity, which she found very amusing, and Meredith had to speak her mind.

'That's a pity,' said her father, 'because we desperately need you in the office. Mary Talbot left this week and it's not easy to replace someone who's been with the firm for eight years. We talked about you helping out anyway, but now it's rather urgent.'

'I presume Joss Hamblyn drove her away,' said Meredith. 'I can't imagine her leaving for any other reason.' She was making an issue of it, and couldn't understand herself.

'Mary's mother had a stroke on Wednesday,' her mother said quietly. 'It looks like she'll want a lot of nursing and Mary insists she can cope rather than let the old lady be admitted to hospital. She's got a lot of friends who'll rally round.'

Meredith felt awful. 'I'm sorry,' she apologised. 'I didn't know, and of course I'll help in the office. How about starting Monday?'

'That's my girl!' said Howard. He was a handsome man in his mid-fifties with dark hair turned an elegant silver at the temples. He had kept a youthful waistline and wore immaculate clothes, so that even in casual things he always looked well dressed. 'You and Joss'll get along fine after a day or two.'

'But why did he deliberately mislead me?' she demanded, indignation rising in her just at the recollection.

'Like your father said, he probably thought it was a good joke,' said Julia.

'That man wouldn't know how to joke. And why does he have his sister and all those children there? Hasn't she got a husband?'

'Ian Munro is a civil engineer out in Saudi Arabia. Ellen came home to have the baby and she can't rejoin him because there's too much political unrest in the part of the country where he's working.' Her mother poured out coffee and handed it across the table. 'Darling, you're much too thin, and we must get some colour back in your cheeks. You look in need of some country air.'

Meredith shook off her annoyance and smiled ruefully at her parents. 'All right, I shouldn't have let Joss Hamblyn get under my skin.'

'No, you shouldn't.'

Lesson one, she thought, don't criticise the new partner. He was obviously a favourite. If she wanted to settle back here she would have to feel her way carefully for a while, learn how things had gone during her absence. She'd known it wouldn't be easy. The original break had been too traumatic.

'Joss is a fine man,' said Howard, 'and his sister is the sweetest little creature, your mother'll tell you. She's been like another daughter to her. They fitted in here straight away, as if they belonged, and I'm very lucky to have such a competent partner. He's only thirty-two, but he's had a lot of experience and was very highly recommended.' He paused and looked at his wife, as if seeking assurance before going on. She gave an almost imperceptible nod. 'But there's one thing it's only fair to tell you straight away, Meredith. It may shed light on why Joss was a bit offhand with you.'

'Don't tell me ... he resents having the boss's daughter foisted on him. He practically said as much.'

'No, I don't think it has anything to do with that.' Her father cleared his throat. 'I'm not his boss. Joss is very independent and extremely well qualified. What you probably don't know is that he handled the divorce case for Mac Loring's second wife, Corinne, and accredited himself very well indeed.'

So that was it! The treacherous swine! He'd wormed his way in with that ace up his sleeve, knowing the Paxtons were suckers for anyone who supported their anti-Loring policies. And he had had the effrontery to condemn her on principle for her connection with the Lorings. Meredith felt sick. Oh, she remembered Corinne Loring, a very beautiful fortune-hunter who thought she could twist Piers's father round her little finger, but he had been more than a match for her.

She was breathing too quickly. Before answering she had to calm down and choose her words carefully, or the situation would be little better than it had been on the day she left. She felt as if she had come into a wasps nest.

'All I needed was a stick to fan the flames,' she said at last. 'Thanks for the warning.'

It was a round table, but it seemed to Meredith that her parents sat close together and she was still on probation, in spite of their enthusiastic welcome. They looked at each other and there was worry in their eyes.

'Meredith, there's no point in avoiding talk of Piers,' said Howard. 'Much better to clear the air once and for all. Your mother and I were very sorry indeed about what happened, not only because it meant *you* were hurt, but because it was a tragic waste of a young, gifted life. We may not have approved of him, but we would never have wished him ill, as well you know. He was showing himself to be rather more than the brash young man we assumed him to be from his parentage, and we regret the pride that kept us from admitting it when he was alive. Will you let us try to make amends?'

'What amends?' she asked. 'If you're still as bitter towards Mac then I can't begin to forget. I'm fond of him. And you may as well know, if you hadn't guessed before, that I was in love with Piers. I loved him when I went away to work with him. Do you think I would have let any other reason split our family the way it did?'

'Oh, Meredith,' her mother sighed, 'what a sorry mess! Darling, let's not spoil your homecoming when we've longed for it so much. We understand how you felt about Piers and we'll say nothing to upset you. Talk about him if you need to, but please, respect our feelings for . . . well, for the rest of his family.'

'Don't worry, Mummy, my grief has been a very private matter, and it'll stay that way. Now, what's to be done about my car up on the hill?'

The evening had been something of an ordeal and she was glad when it was over, but she was happy the way things were turning out. It hadn't been nearly such a difficult homecoming as she had feared. If it wasn't for that abominable man Hamblyn being around she could have said she was looking forward to a more peaceful life, but she could imagine fireworks when their paths next crossed. She'd face that problem when she came to it, but it wasn't a pleasant prospect.

Her bedroom was rather special. She had chosen the décor herself before she left home, and seeing everything unchanged gave her a feeling of security. The walls were a dusty pink, with cushions and curtains of palest green and pink to tone, with a darker pink bedcover. Even the house plants she had grouped in a dark corner flourished more luxuriously than before, their dark shiny leaves thriving better there than they would have done in direct sunlight. The colour scheme complemented the cane furniture and did away with any Victorian stuffiness which still lingered in some parts of the house.

Though it was still only May the weather was mild and daylight was reluctant to fade completely. There was a cherry tree outside her window which tapped the glass if the wind was high, but tonight the leaves were motionless and only an occasional petal from the faded blossom floated down to the lawn beneath like a snowflake. Meredith opened the window and caught one in her hand, then leaned with her elbows on the sill.

Her room was at the back of the old Victorian house with its ivy-covered walls, and the garden stretched

down almost as far as the eye could see to the stables
where she had once kept a pony. It was too dark to see
them now, but she visualised the old stone building
which had been like a sanctuary when she needed one.
Her father had threatened to pull down the stables and
get planning permission for a couple of houses. Not
that he would have been likely to get it, because there
was no access other than by a footpath which led up to
the moors, but he enjoyed teasing her. Tomorrow she
would go and see if the stables still held the same magic.

Before going to bed she decided to empty her case and
hang up her things, but when she lifted the lid and saw the
state of the clothes that Joss Hamblyn had squashed in, a
fresh wave of annoyance caught up with her.

'Ohhh! You hateful man!' she exclaimed, out loud,
clenching her fists with a desire to strike him. Good job
he wasn't around!

She started folding everything, making neat piles
ready to be transferred to the drawers, but it would be
impossible to wear any of the pastel silk underwear
until it had been ironed, and in a rare fit of frustration
she picked up a stack of it and flung it across the room,
watching it cascade down like silk from a magician's
hat. It was a pointless thing to do, but it made her feel
better.

Midway down the case was a photograph of Piers in
an embossed silver frame which she had wrapped in a
cashmere sweater for safe keeping. It was a press photo,
enlarged from a newspaper picture, and was the best
likeness of him she had seen. The cameraman had
caught him as he was talking, his expression animated,
every line of him vibrating with that restless energy that
had been so characteristic. Piers had never been still
for a minute. Every kiss had been a fleeting rapture
with the promise of endless time ahead in which to
linger over love.

Meredith had loved him from the moment they met. Piers had been reading Mathematics and his future was mapped out for him. Armed with a degree, he was to go into commerce, but the prospect appalled him, and when Meredith was introduced to him at a party he was already planning his business empire. He had a brilliant mind, but within the first hour of knowing him she could tell he would never be happy in some static job, closed in by four walls. He was too vital. From the moment he started dating her she had difficulty keeping up with him. His ideas sent him off investigating avenues of the rag trade she had never heard of, and she found if she went along she always needed a pad and pencil to make notes. The next step was a borrowed typewriter in her room in the evenings, and her own studies suffered, but at least she was with Piers.

'I know he's gorgeous,' one of her friends said, 'but how do you put up with him? He's obsessed with becoming a tycoon before he's twenty-five and never talks of anything else.'

'It's different when we're alone,' she explained. But she was kidding herself as well. For a while he might kiss her, even fondle her experimentally, but he was too preoccupied for romance and reverted to trade and markets at the first opportunity. The only figures which really interested him were the ones on paper that he could calculate methodically. But he succeeded in infecting her with his enthusiasm.

'Meredith, you're a cinch for big business,' he had said, late one evening. 'I've never met a girl who could follow my way of thinking the way you do. I never want to lose you.'

Her heart had leapt. He was going to say he loved her, and all the waiting and perseverence with financial matters had paid off.

'Why should you even think of losing me?'

He took her in his arms. 'I was hoping you'd say that. You see, I'm giving up university at the end of term and I'm ready to start out on my own. But I need you with me. Are you willing to sacrifice your chance of a degree to come in with me?'

'Oh, Piers, you know I am!' Her heart was beating crazily.

'Then I'll work on my old man and the bank, and if you can manage to chip in with a bit of cash all the better. We'll need every penny we can get. We'll be supplying our first store within a couple of months. I couldn't do it without you, Meredith. You'll have to be personal secretary, assistant, adviser, the lot, until we get into the big time.'

She was hooked. Too late to back down and say she wanted marriage. Piers didn't have time for marriage, and if he returned her love it was in his own way, with praise and acknowledgement of her help. Her reward was the mushroom growth of the Piers Loring Group. She had met, and liked, his father, mixed well with his few close friends, and smiled at the glamorous females who flitted in and out of his working life, secure in the knowledge that she was the only girl who really mattered to him. But loving him was like chasing sunbeams. Just when she had thought perfect happiness was within her grasp another cloud would come and dash it away. Perhaps it would always have been like that.

She put the photograph on her dressing table and finished unpacking. The drawers, which had been plenty big enough for her things before she went away, were now overflowing, and she dreaded to think where she was going to find room for the rest of her stuff when it came. She would have to buy another wardrobe.

When she had unknotted her hair and brushed it

down, she took stock of herself in the mirror. Her
mother was right; she looked decidedly peaky, and for
the first time she admitted to herself that it would be
nice not to have to keep up the phenomenal pressure
that success demanded. But she was glad, too, that
there was a job for her. After working flat out for nine
and ten hours a day, idleness was unthinkable, and she
didn't want to have too much time to spare to become
maudlin over Piers.

The weekend passed smoothly. If there was any
jarring note at all it was the continual singing of Ellen
Munro's praises. It seemed as if her mother couldn't
stop talking about her, and after a while it became
irritating, though Meredith tried not to show it. The
poor girl would probably have been very embarrassed if
she had known how she was held up as a paragon of all
the virtues. There had to be a flaw in her somewhere, or
she wouldn't be human.

'You haven't said if you like the new decor in the
lounge,' Julia said, on the Saturday morning.

Meredith looked round the room with fresh eyes.
'You've got new curtains,' she said, admiring the off-
white linen that brightened the place considerably.
Embroidered cushions she hadn't seen before brought
colour to the old leather chesterfield, and the wing
chairs had been covered in an attractive chintz.

'I'm glad you like them. They were Ellen's choice and
she helped me to make them.'

'Ellen!' That accounted for the taste in chintz which
was similar to the design she had seen so recently at
Eden Farm. 'Did she make the cushion covers, too?'

'Oh, no. There was a handicraft sale in the village
and I bought them there. Ellen organised the sale,
though. It was in aid of handicapped children. She's a
marvellous girl, Meredith.'

Meredith agreed wholeheartedly, but that was only

the beginning. After several more references to her mother's fondness for Ellen, she found herself experiencing a completely new pain, quite unlike the physical ache in her ankle which was gradually easing away, and different from anything she had known before. It attacked her so unexpectedly she didn't recognise it at first, but after a few minutes she knew it could only be attributed to jealousy. In a way it was her own fault she had been usurped in her mother's affections. She hadn't been around to show her the love she needed and when Ellen came along with a similar need and like interests it was only natural that the two should take to each other. She ought to be glad, because she had forfeited the right to her mother's exclusive love when she made the decision to put Piers first. It was a fact she had to accept, but it didn't lessen the hurt brought on by the discovery.

'I often mind the children for her,' Julia Paxton said. 'They really are very sweet.'

'*You* mind them!' Meredith couldn't believe it. Her mother was unstinting in her social work for the community, but had always drawn the line at being involved with other people's children, declaring she hadn't enough patience and dreaded sticky fingers over everything. 'Surely you don't have those two rough little boys up here as well? What on earth made her take up fostering? She must be mad!'

'They're nice children really. A bit rough, as you say, but it's only to be expected. They come from broken homes in the East End of London, and they hadn't even seen a green field until they came here. They're quite well behaved on the whole.'

'They must be for you to say so, Mummy. I bet they're too scared of you to say anything!'

Julia laughed. 'Well, I make them tow the line. Ellen does, too. It's her ambition to start a holiday centre for deprived children, and I know she would make a splendid job of it.'

'And what about Joss Hamblyn?' asked Meredith. 'Doesn't he mind having his house filled with hordes of children?'

She couldn't keep the malice out of her voice.

'Joss is quite extraordinary with them,' said Julia, with a gentle smile. 'The more he shouts, the more they love it, and they follow him everywhere. I laughed at him the other day and said he couldn't have had a more suitable name. He's like the Pied Piper of Hamelin. Children have an instinct for these things. And, of course, Ellen works *so* hard. I don't suppose Joss knows the children are there half the time.'

That was when Meredith's patience wore so thin she felt compelled to raise an objection.

'Honestly, Mummy, you'd think no one else ever did as much as Ellen Munro! All she does is run a house and look after a family. It's what most women do, and it's the natural thing. I've been working pretty hard myself, and believe me, there's a lot of strain goes into building up a business like . . .' she hesitated before mentioning Piers, then decided his name must be used in conversation naturally right from the start, '. . . like the one Piers created. Some nights I felt too exhausted to sleep. My brain was far too active.'

They were sorting out the store cupboard, making room for Julia's jampots and putting anything surplus in a box ready for the local scouts jumble sale, but she put down the jar she had been holding and held out her arms to her daughter.

'My poor darling,' she said, unexpectedly smothering Meredith in maternal love, 'I have been going on a bit, haven't I? And I can't begin to tell you how happy I am to have you back with us. No one could *ever* take your place.' Then she held her away from her with a sly smile. 'But one day, my girl, you'll learn it isn't all honey looking after children.'

Meredith grinned in reply. 'Not me,' she said. 'I intend to be a dedicated career woman.'

By Monday morning her ankle had almost returned to normal, apart from being coloured a startling blue and yellow. To disguise it she wore navy-blue tights with flat shoes which looked good with a pleated blue skirt. She was tempted to leave her long hair loose, but she needed all the dignity she could muster to face Joss Hamblyn, so she coiled it swiftly and anchored it with more pins than usual, shaking her head to make sure it was firm.

Her father took her down early to the village and dropped her at the garage to collect her car. The Stag was ready for her and already being admired by a group of boys on their way to school. She patted it lovingly and went to thank the mechanic.

'My pleasure, Miss Paxton,' he said. 'Nice to see you home. Sure is a super car you got now. What happened to the old banger you used to bring in here regular, like?'

She laughed, a glow of pleased surprise lighting her face. 'Oh, Ted, fancy you remembering! Do you know, it nearly broke my heart to part with it, but the poor old thing couldn't cope with London traffic.'

'Well, this little beauty complements the owner, if I may say so. You're looking prettier than ever. A bit pale, mind, but that's only to be expected after the bad time you had. We was all mighty sorry. Still, a few sunny days down here'll soon put the colour back in your cheeks.'

Meredith actually blushed at the flattery. She'd forgotten how friendly and nice village people were.

'Better take it for a spin round the block to make sure everything's okay,' Ted advised. 'If not I'll have another look at it. Can't have you walking miles and spraining the other ankle.'

Gosh, how news got around! 'I'm sure it'll be just fine,' said Meredith.

She drove through the main street, feeling as if all eyes were on her. She's back, then, she imagined everyone saying. The Paxton girl's back. Sad she ran out of luck! No, that was what Joss Hamblyn had said, and he hadn't meant it kindly. Surely the people of this lovely Devon village wouldn't be any less sympathetic than Ted at the garage had been. It was just as well she hadn't come home straight after Piers's death. Sympathy then would have been too hard to take.

The office hadn't changed at all. It was in a row of Georgian houses which had once been private dwellings, but they had all been converted into shops or offices and formed a picturesque part of the main road through Edencombe. Bow-fronted windows looked out on a wide grass verge that sloped down to the road, and the original oak door of number five closed behind her with a resounding thud as she went inside, sending a shiver of apprehension down her spine. She stood a moment in the hall, the musty smell which had been synonymous with the place for as long as she could remember seeming stronger than ever.

'Meredith!' her father called.

She went into his room, and there was a certain comfort about the sameness of everything. The gold writing on the window announcing that this was a solicitor's office was still as difficult to read back to front, and though the leather chairs had been re-upholstered, familiar dents and ink marks remained on the vast writing desk, and the bookshelves sported very few new volumes. No, nothing had changed except the addition to the nameplate above the front entrance, which now read 'Paxton, Smith and Hamblyn.'

'We're early yet,' said Howard. 'When Betty comes she'll start showing you the ropes. How do you feel about throwing your lot in with us for a while, now you've got here, I mean?'

'Nervous,' said Meredith.

He gave her shoulder a reassuring squeeze. 'Nonsense! After the work you've been doing the job here'll be a snip.' He paused, weighing up the problem from her point of view. 'Tell you what, shall I ask Betty to go in with Joss today, and you can work for me? I guess I can put up with you!'

She smiled at him gratefully, but refused. 'Thanks, but if I'm going to be working with Joss Hamblyn that's where I'll start. No sense prolonging the agony. Besides, I know what a sacrifice it would be for you to lose Betty even for a day.'

Like the ink marks on the desk, it seemed as if Betty had been there for ever. She could remember being brought into her father's office before she even started school and Betty had kept sweets for her in a special drawer. How could she bear to have stayed in a job so long? It was lucky she had never married, or her father would have had to train someone else to take on important slices of his work.

'You'll like Joss when you get to know him properly,' Howard was saying. His mouth quirked up lopsidedly into a grin that showed he was still a very attractive man. 'Most women find him irresistible, for some reason.'

'Well, *I* can resist him without any trouble at all.' Meredith said shortly. 'If that's the mail, Daddy, I'll take it over to his office and get it sorted before he comes in.' She paused. 'By the way, I can't go on calling you Daddy at work. How do you fancy me using your first name?'

'I fancy that just fine. It'll knock ten years off my

age, and that can't be bad.' When she tweaked his ear
playfully, he gave her a quick hug. 'It *is* good to have
you home, Merry.'

She crossed the hall, feeling chilly in spite of the
mildness of the spring day. Joss Hamblyn had taken
over the litigation side of the practice and his room
was at the back of the house, but though she knew
he hadn't arrived she delayed entering for several
seconds. She had managed to put up a mental barrier
over the weekend, refusing to think about him, but
now it had to be pulled down, and she was not
looking forward to it. She didn't want to touch his
books and papers, and she knew instinctively that
whatever she did in the office this morning would be
wrong. Anticipating it, her nerves began to tingle.
Then she muttered, 'So what!' under her breath,
turned the handle and went inside.

Ellen Munro had been busy here, too. Evidence of
her artistic flare abounded. The walls were a delicate
mushroom shade, as was the ceiling, with the exception
of the stucco work which had been left white and now
became a feature of the room. The curtains were grey
velvet, and an armchair was covered in pink floral
material that went well with the grey carpet, but the old
marble fireplace and original oak desk were unchanged.
It was a pleasant room, looking out on a walled garden,
and Meredith realised how nice it must have been when
this was a family residence. It made her father's room
seem cold and inhospitable by comparison, and a new
indignation welled up in her.

Joss Hamblyn had everything going for him, didn't
he? He had obviously established himself already as a
fine solicitor. With clients like Corinne Loring winning
a good reputation for him it was no wonder he could
afford a house like Eden Farm. It was surprising that
Edencombe was big enough for him. There couldn't be

that many important divorce or custody cases around here to bring him further notoriety.

Betty came and helped her with the mail and explained some of the routine procedures. Dear Betty, looking more like a schoolmarm than ever, thought it grand having Meredith around.

'Keep your father in his place,' she said, with a twinkle. 'And this one can do with tough handling. Mary was too soft on him,'

'Mary was soft on Joss Hamblyn? I can't imagine it.'

'Oh, everyone is,' said Betty.

He was very late arriving. Perhaps he never bothered to come before ten o'clock. Meredith had never known her father unpunctual and she found dilatory behaviour inexcusable. When he finally came in there was a churning feeling in her stomach, and the anger that had been boiling up ever since her mother had put her right as to his identity could no longer be contained. As soon as he came through the door antagonism sparked between them, and his attempt at a gracious welcome was lost in electrified awareness of mutual aversion.

'Why didn't you let me know who you were?' she demanded. 'You let me make a fool of myself and all the while you were laughing at me. It was despicable!'

He came over to the desk, his face darkening. 'It's customary to say good morning before you launch into a tirade, Miss Paxton. Were manners not necessary at the Piers Loring Group? As it seems we shall be meeting here daily perhaps we can get it right at the start.'

'If this is the time you always come in I shall feel inclined to make it good afternoon,' she said sarcastically, with a deliberate glance at the clock.

He ignored the inference and picked up his letters. 'I take it you've been through these and set aside anything important.'

'There's one that needs your attention. I've put it

with the relevant file on the case. My father has already seen to his urgent business.'

She was baiting him, watching for his reaction, and she didn't know why she was doing it. Joss put both hands on the desk and leaned towards her, his eyes cold as granite. A shiver went through her and she pulled the lilac cashmere jacket round her shoulders, her fingers gripping it with unnecessary strength.

'If you're trying to tell me something, it doesn't cut any ice,' he said, his voice heavy with sarcasm. 'I'm not impressed at having the secretary of a jumped-up millionaire coming here to run *my* office. Now, if you'd bothered to look at my diary first thing this morning, as Mary always did, you would have seen that I had an appointment at nine o'clock to see someone on Sid Frank's behalf. He's the landlord of the New Inn, if you remember.'

'How convenient! Are your first appointments always on licensed premises?'

The retort was out before she had time to consider the inadvisability of it. She had said the first ridiculous thing that came into her head, and in different circumstances it could have been a joke. Joss Hamblyn didn't take it as one. He came round the desk and caught her arm in an iron grip.

'I won't tolerate insolence from anyone,' he snapped. 'I don't care whether you're Howard's daughter or who you are, if you speak to me like that again, you're out!'

The jacket fell from her shoulders and the fingers round her arm had masculine strength that gave no quarter, but she wouldn't cry out even when the pressure felt like a tourniquet. She looked at his hand, then raised her eyes to meet his and was lost somewhere in their green depths. They bored into her, their intensity weakening her resistance, and she had the curious feeling that this man intended to dominate her. She ought to have seized the opportunity his ultimatum had created and used it as a means of escape, but those eyes held her captive, and almost against her will she found herself apologising.

'I'm sorry,' she said. 'It's the sort of stupid remark I would have made to Piers and he would have laughed.'

Her voice had softened and he accepted the apology reluctantly. His hand dropped from her arm.

'When we're on the same terms as you were with Piers Loring I'll allow you to make Loring-type quips. Until then, please remember this is my office and you are an employee.'

'What makes you think we'll ever be on such terms?' she asked. 'Piers and I had a very special relationship.'

'I know.' Joss went over to the window and even the line of his back was arrogant. The grey suit he wore gave him the right professional air, and a severity she couldn't associate with the spell he was supposed to cast on women and children. But though she hated to admit it, there had been a certain rakish charm about him in open-necked shirt and corduroy pants. 'I know a lot more about you than you think, Meredith.'

'Indeed!'

She stood very still, sensing danger. The air quivered with it, and she moved to the centre of the room as if afraid of being cornered. Her palms felt clammy and her breathing was fast and shallow, but she set her head high and waited for what was to come, giving him no encouragement.

Joss turned slowly. 'Don't worry, anything I learn is strictly confidential.'

'Why should I worry? If you've been trying to dig up anything shady I'm sure you were unsuccessful. And why should you want to pry into my private affairs?'

He was blotting out some of the sunlight and his tall figure cast a shadow across the desk. He filled her with loathing and a dreadful disquiet, though it was difficult to define the reason. Then he smiled unexpectedly and she was thrown into greater confusion because the gesture was boyishly beguiling.

'You're right,' he agreed. 'Your private life is your own. But I'm very attached to your parents and it makes me sad to think of the way you intended to deceive them.'

Her tongue passed nervously over her top lip. 'And what further crime do you think I had in mind?'

She was hedging, trying to stall him, because there was no doubt Joss Hamblyn had discovered the one fact she had hoped to keep secret from her parents. Damn him!

His eyes held hers mercilessly as he said: 'I know, my dear Meredith, that you were on the point of marrying Piers Loring.'

CHAPTER THREE

MEREDITH was trembling and she knew Joss could see it. The shock of the statement went deep, because the one thing she had wanted more than anything in the world was to be married to Piers. They had kept their plans secret because she had been afraid her father might try to stop the wedding, though he would have had to know once it was an accomplished fact. But it hadn't taken place, and she had decided it was unnecessary to hurt her parents more by letting them know how close it had been.

'I don't doubt your friend Corinne gave you that piece of information,' she said. 'Discretion isn't one of her virtues.'

'Piers told her himself.'

'In self-defence, I shouldn't wonder.' She gave him a straight look. 'He didn't care much for his stepmother and he wouldn't have taken her into his confidence.'

Joss sat down at his desk. 'She told *me* because she thought someone here ought to know about it before the news became public, and she was right. You couldn't have kept it secret, you know.'

Meredith clasped her arms round her tightly, warding off the pain that memories brought. She hadn't let herself think about it, much less talk about it, since the crash, but this man had touched on that raw subject with all the cruelty of an unfeeling moron.

'I wouldn't have tried,' she said. 'But there's no need to hurt my parents now by telling them what might have been.' She paused and took a breath. 'The day Piers died should have been our wedding day, but with predictable timing something more important cropped up and he had to fly to Paris instead, so the ceremony was postponed. It wasn't the first time.'

Joss eyed her keenly, witnessed her grief, and the first hint of compassion crept into his voice.

'I'm sorry, Meredith. I shoot off my mouth sometimes when I shouldn't,' he said. He picked up a paperweight and balanced it in his hand, weighing up his next move. When it came he was still scathing. 'That was a pretty ghastly thing to happen to any girl. But to be that close to marrying into a fortune must have made it even worse.'

The prickling of indignation was like a bombardment of pins against her skin.

'I hope you meant that remark as a misplaced form of sympathy, because if not I take exception to it. It was cynical and not very clever.'

'So money had nothing to do with the wedding plans,' said Joss sceptically. 'Perhaps that's just as well. It's easy to fall off the top of a ladder, and Piers Loring got there a bit too fast for safety to my way of thinking. You might have had to pick up the pieces.'

'I would have done that, too,' she said. 'But there was no fear of it happening, I assure you. I had complete faith in him. Why else would I have invested all *my* money at the outset?'

'And you've come out of it no poorer that you went in, I'm sure.'

Meredith wanted to strike that handsome face, but the satisfaction wouldn't be worth the loss of dignity and would only weaken her position. He was taking pleasure in trying to annoy her, but she was not going to rise to the bait. Better to stay coldly aloof.

'If it bugs you that I'm doing someone else out of a job I'll be happy to resign before I even begin,' she said, keeping her tone level with difficulty. 'It was my father's idea that I should be your temporary secretary. He thought it would benefit you and be good therapy for me, but obviously he was wrong on both counts.' She waited, half turning her head, but she was afraid to take her eyes off him in case he attacked again while she was unprepared. Then she went on: 'Just to set the record straight, and before the subject is closed for good, let me tell you I would have married Piers while we were still at university if he'd asked me, when we had nothing but driving ambition. So whatever gold-digging ideas you may have had about me, forget them.'

Joss looked faintly abashed. 'Okay, so I guess you loved the guy after all.' He stood up, acknowledging her right to be resentful of interference, but he didn't leave it there. When he spoke again his voice was soft, almost caring. 'Meredith, has it ever occurred to you that you might have had a lucky escape? That marriage to Piers Loring might have made you very unhappy indeed?'

She met his eyes warily, distrusting the concern. 'What makes you say that?'

'Corinne always said there was something odd about Piers. He never had time for anything except work.'

He had succeeded in whipping up anger. She was furious.

'If you believe Corinne Loring, you'll believe anything!' she stormed. 'I've seen her trying to get round Piers and becoming vindictive when it didn't work.'

'Are you forgetting I'm a solicitor, and a good one at that? It's my job to judge whether people are telling the truth,' he said coldly.

'Then how is it you let her blind you? Were you *that* infatuated?' She was governed by emotion now, speaking out involuntarily with the intention of hurting. It wasn't often she was goaded enough to retaliate, but

Joss Hamblyn qualified as the most loathsome man she had met in a long while.

'We'll leave her out of the discussion,' he said, his eyes narrowing dangerously.

'Why?' countered Meredith. 'Why should you object to hearing things about Corinne when you're intent on degrading Piers?'

'You're prejudiced, Meredith.'

'I've every right to be. Piers isn't alive to defend himself.' What was wrong with them, sparring like enemies when they hardly even knew each other? If Joss had said a civil word to her in their brief acquaintance it had passed unnoticed. 'I can't stay and listen to any more,' she said, slipping on her jacket. 'I don't know why you've got such a low opinion of me. What have I done to you?'

Joss got up and came round the desk, lifting his hands hesitantly, and she took a step backwards. The thought of any contact with him filled her with revulsion. Suddenly he gave a wry smile and the merest acquiescent nod, accepting her question as valid.

'What *have* you done to me?' he asked, the words sounding strangely perplexed. 'For some reason you seem to bring out the worst in me. How would it be if we made a fresh start? I'll come in the door and introduce myself properly and we'll behave just like ordinary people. I'm not usually so boorish, I promise you.'

'I'm glad to hear it,' she said, and was tempted to believe the gesture of contrition was genuine. But it was too late for him to put on the charm and expect her to be impressed. She made an effort and composed herself, aware that she must meet his overture halfway. 'If you feel that we *can* work together in a reasonably amicable atmosphere I'm willing to start again, but if you really don't want me here, please say so outright, and I'll leave now.'

She was a tall, slender girl, but she had to look up at Joss when he was near.

'I *do* want you here, Meredith,' he said, 'and not only because I know it's what your father wants. Please stay.'

He stretched out his hand, and she found herself taking it, her own lost in his firm grip. A curious warmth flowed between them which was not unpleasant, and though the hardness of his fingers made her rings bite into the skin she found an almost masochistic satisfaction in the sharp pain. So this was a kind of truce. Suddenly he gave a dazzling smile which lit up his whole face and took her breath away. If this had really been their first meeting she would have felt dizzy at the reception.

The rest of the morning passed swiftly. Joss had cancelled any further appointments so that he was free to explain the way he liked things done, and by lunchtime Meredith's head was buzzing. She didn't need to be told how good he was at his job; the work he did spoke for itself. The receptionist and the typist in the outer office were plainly in awe of him, and even Betty seemed to treat him with a certain deference that was quite surprising. Meredith raised her eyebrows and wondered what they would have made of the slanging match that had taken place earlier. Obviously the female staff respected Joss Hamblyn's air of authority and never crossed him. Well, from now on she would be equally remote and refer only to the work in hand.

She decided not to go home for lunch but to take the car and find somewhere to sit quietly while her head cleared; an hour of peaceful solitude by a stretch of water was what she needed. She looked in on her father and told him where she was going, then set off.

The river hurried down from the moors, bubbling and frothing over rocks until it reached Edencombe, where it slowed to a more sedate pace and broadened out round the eastern side of the village. At the end of the main street it flowed beneath a mediaeval seven-arched bridge of mellow stone, and a mile beyond that was a pull-in where parking was allowed for anyone wanting to walk through woodland that bordered the water. Meredith parked there, glad that no other cars were around, and spent several minutes just enjoying the soothing quietness.

She wondered whether Joss Hamblyn liked the countryside, or whether, like Piers, he had no time for dreaming beside a river. Piers would have been looking at his watch, anxious to be going, though he might just have considered a walk through the trees. He had been loose-limbed, the athletic type, wiry beside a man of Joss's stature. Just thinking about him made her feel guilty about doing nothing. He had had that effect on people, making them get up and look busy because his vitality put them to shame. She got out of the car, locked it, and set off down the incline to the river.

There were shouts of childish laughter coming from downstream. She remembered how she had loved to come here as a child and play in the shallows, no amusement better than setting off with a fishing net and jamjar in the hope of catching minnows, a pack of sandwiches for later. Some of the minnows and sticklebacks had found their way into the goldfish pond at home and had actually thrived. Meredith smiled to herself. How far off those carefree days seemed now; before boarding school and university; before Piers. Funny how her time with him had become symbolic, the milestone in her life by which she measured the difference between past and present.

She sat down on a bank and slipped off her shoes. It had been a mistake to come so far. Her ankle throbbed and was swelling slightly again, so she reached down and soaked her handkerchief in the clear, icy water not yet touched by the spring sunshine, and bound it tightly round the sprain. But the throbbing merely shifted to another part of her body, becoming the familiar heartache she thought she had at last learned to control. Joss was to blame. He, of all people, had stated the one fact she had always dreaded hearing, yet he hadn't known Piers personally. It was ironic.

Had Corinne taken malicious pleasure in saying there was something odd about Piers, or had she been speaking the truth? Doubts which had clouded Meredith's mind more than once had now been put into words, and she couldn't ignore them. Nor could she deny the disappointment and anguish Piers had caused her on many occasions. It was true he had always been working to the hilt, sometimes to the point of exhaustion, but he had never asked to stay at her flat when they had had a late night, never attempted to make love to her even though they intended to marry, and she was embarrassed to remember how she had sometimes longed to persuade him. On the day he died, the third postponement of a hurried register office wedding, she had acknowledged that Piers was afraid of marriage, and had been prepared to call it off altogether when he got back from Paris, for his sake, not hers. Perhaps Joss was right, damn him. If she had gone through with it she might already be regretting it, so maybe she had had a lucky escape. It didn't help matters, though, that he had been the one to point it out.

She wandered back slowly by a different route which was easier on her ankle, and she came to the beck. It chuckled over smooth stones, dark as bitter chocolate, dipping deeper to the river at the bottom, and branches lay in criss-cross patterns that the water and wildlife had created. A slippery black shape squirmed up on to a rock, then slithered back into a pool where the water eddied, not appearing again until the beck shallowed. She smiled. It was years since she had seen an otter and it was great to know nothing disturbed him. A bird flew down on to the wet patch where the otter had played, winking at her with a bright, beady eye, and fish incessantly jumped. Gradually the peacefulness of that lovely place seeped into her and she felt able to cope with the rest of the day.

She climbed up through a grove of larch trees which allowed dappled sunlight to brighten the soft earth like a carpet under her feet, and just as she reached the road she heard children's voices again. They were close now, close enough to be round her car, and there was no mistaking the cockney accents. As she came into the open there was a yell, and two boys ran off as fast as they could go, disappearing into the trees like rabbits into burrows. But not before she had recognised Shaun and Gary, the children being fostered by Ellen Munro.

'Come back here this minute!' she shouted, sensing trouble before she had proof of it, but it was a waste of breath. They had no intention of answering a summons like that.

When she looked at her car their reason for haste was patently obvious. Three of the tyres were completely flat, and the fourth was sinking to the rim with a sigh of resignation. Meredith did more than sigh. She shouted at the top of her voice, so angry she felt like using expletives she had never used before in her life. It was probably what they would have understood anyway. There was no movement from the trees, not the slightest stirring of the undergrowth, and only the echo of her own infuriated cry came back to her. She clenched her fists and bit hard on her lips.

There was nothing she could do about it. She walked round the car, investigating to see if there was any more damage, and picked up a green knitted scarf that one of the boys had dropped. She folded it and put it in the top of her bag, wishing another motorist would pull in, but the few car drivers on the road flashed by without a second glance. She felt like bursting into tears, but that would have solved nothing. The only thing to do was start walking and hope she could reach the telephone box about half a mile away before her ankle gave out altogether.

She had intended phoning home to ask her father to drive out and pick her up, but changed her mind. Let Jess take responsibility for his two delinquents. It necessitated getting on to directory enquiries for the number because Joss Hamblyn hadn't been at Eden Farm long enough to be listed, but he was the one who ought to do the running about when those little hooligans were his responsibility.

'What on earth is the matter with you, girl?' he demanded, not liking his lunch disturbed. 'Can't you be out alone for five minutes without calling for help! And why ring me?'

'The vandals you so righteously imported into Edencombe have let down the tyres of my car,' snapped Meredith. 'I don't see why my father should have to use his petrol to come and pick me up, and I can't walk back.'

'I presume you mean Shaun and Gary. How do you know it was them?' Joss asked. 'It could have been any boys.'

'I saw them, and heard them.'

Silence for a second, in which she could visualise his brows drawing thunderously together. Then: 'I'll be there in five minutes,' he said, and slammed the phone down.

She waited by the phone box, catching a glimpse of herself in the glass panels as she closed the door. Her cheeks were flushed, and low branches had dragged

pins out of her hair when she walked by the river,
setting free long wisps of it and creating something of a
bird's nest effect. She hardly looked like the immaculate
Miss Paxton who had reported for duty at the offices of
Paxton, Smith and Hamblyn that morning, and when
she glanced down at the handkerchief still tied round
her ankle she knew she was looking a positive wreck.
She stared at her reflection in dismay, preparing to do
battle with Joss the moment he arrived, but then the
most unexpected thing happened. Laughter bubbled up
in her for the first time in weeks and she found herself
giving way to helpless giggles, which had to be
repressed when she saw Joss's car approaching. It
wouldn't do to let him know she had seen the funny
side of the situation.

'Are you all right?' he asked, anxiously, seeing tears
on her cheeks. 'They didn't attack you, for Pete's sake?'

'Of course not,' she said.

He pushed open the car door from inside and she got
in. There must have been a magic quality about the
woods that had cast a spell over her, because only a few
hours ago she would have been in a foul mood over the
immobilisation of her car, but for a short time she had
relaxed with childhood memories which had helped
her put the devilment of two small boys in better
perspective. Meredith Paxton, you're beginning to feel
human again at last, she thought, and covered her
mouth with her hand as a fresh wave of laughter
threatened. There was hope for her yet.

Joss eyed her sharply. 'You look a bit of a mess,' he
commented. No diplomacy from this arrogant male.
'Are you sure you're all right?' When she couldn't hold
back another giggle the sharpness turned to amazement.
'Have you had any lunch?'

'No, I haven't,' she said, 'but I'm not lightheaded, if
that's what you're thinking. When I saw my car with

four flat tyres I was absolutely livid, but I've come to the conclusion it isn't worth raising my blood pressure any higher. I've been taking life much too seriously. If you could have seen those boys' faces when I suddenly appeared! They were like frightened rabbits.'

'They'll be punished,' Joss promised.

'No,' said Meredith, 'let them get away with it this time. I'll phone Ted at the garage as soon as I get back and ask him to do something about the car. Do you think there'll be a third time?'

'Not if I have anything to do with it. And I'm afraid I can't let the boys get away with that kind of prank, whatever you say. You've surprised me.'

'I've surprised myself,' she admitted.

He hadn't shared her humour and he surveyed her critically. 'You were a fool to go walking so soon after a bad sprain. No wonder that ankle's swollen again! Now, tidy yourself up and we'll go to the Crown for some sandwiches before closing time. *I* haven't had lunch either.'

He gave orders with clipped impatience, trying to put her in her place.

'You sound exactly like Piers,' she said, all thought of laughter evaporating. Piers had never liked a hint of untidiness, and even at weekends he had talked her out of slopping around in a pair of comfortable old jeans. The comparison affected her strangely, and with an abrupt swing of mood she was plunged into a new trough of despair for which she couldn't find an exact reason. 'If you're ashamed of being seen with me as I am you'll have to wait while I use a brush.'

Before he could put the car into gear Meredith pulled the rest of the pins out of her hair. It tumbled free, a thick dark mane that rippled over her shoulders and down her back. With the deftness of experience she slid the brush through it with hard strokes, the bristles singing with the swift movement; then with a tilt of her head the hair swung to her right so that she could gather the weight into her hands and twist it. When strong masculine fingers gripped her wrist, stilling it, she felt as if she was caught in a vice.

'Don't pin it up again,' said Joss.

She turned. The low voice was pitched at a level calculated to weaken her limbs. Before, she had blamed her shoes and the steepness of the road, but this time there was no flippant explanation. She shook her hair back, tucking the front strands behind her ears, and there was a swirling in her head which hadn't come from hard brushing. Somehow she daren't meet his eyes.

'It isn't practical this way,' she protested. 'Piers said I ought to have it cut short.'

'That's the unappreciative kind of comment he was bound to make,' said Joss disgustedly. 'We haven't been in each other's company a day yet, and already the sound of his name is getting up my nose. Is it possible to have a conversation without him coming into it?'

She said nothing, too stunned by his callousness to find an answer, but she moved as far away as possible from him in the confined space and deliberately coiled her hair into a neat topknot in defiance of his request. Joss watched, fascinated. And he laughed.

There was a client waiting for him on his return. It was a girl in a short, tight skirt, with pale lipstick and large ear-rings. She trailed a peevish toddler behind her and carried a baby in her arms.

'He hasn't sent me maintenance for three months,' the girl complained, as Meredith was showing her into the room. 'I shall have to have another solicitor's letter, and it makes me so mad, because there's another slice out of me measly allowance.'

Meredith shut the door sadly, leaving Joss to cope

with the estranged wife and grizzling child. She wondered whether she ought to have offered to look after the children while he spoke to her, but miraculously the crying stopped after a few seconds and the only sound was the clicking of the typewriter in reception.

'Mr Hamblyn has a real way with children,' said Betty, coming up behind her. 'And everyone likes him. Isn't it wonderful?'

The poor woman looked quite smitten, and Meredith smiled, not having the heart to contradict. There must be something about Joss she had missed if a person like Betty, an avowed spinster, went limp and soft-eyed at the sight of him.

There was no doubt about it, Joss Hamblyn was an asset to the partnership, whatever her own sentiments might be. She couldn't imagine her father dealing so patiently with clients who brought along noisy children; but then her father was a conveyancing solicitor, mainly concerned with the sale and purchase of property, so he didn't come in contact with life's heartrending problems in quite the way Joss did. Michael Smith, the third member of the practice, dealt with probate and had patience of a different kind with the old folk and invalids so often in need of his services. When it came to sorting out a contested will there was no one better, but Joss was the one who had had experience of lawsuits and needed a special kind of understanding to judge the pros and cons of marital distress. Perhaps that was why he had never married.

It was halfway through the afternoon when Shaun and Gary appeared, dragging their feet and not too happy about being summoned to the office. Both wore grey school trousers and pullovers, but the younger boy was huddled into a parka which was much too warm for the mild spring day.

'Why haven't you been to school?' Joss asked, making them stand in front of his desk as if he was a headmaster.

Gary was in a patch of sunlight and his short-cropped fair hair gleamed like a halo round his pudgy little face. Shaun had tight black curls which looked impossible to comb, and his small, pinched features were softened by a pair of soulful eyes which he turned upon Gary, obviously used to taking the lead from him.

'We 'ave been to school,' said Gary.

'Not since lunchtime. I've checked,' said Joss. 'So I want to know what you can tell me about four flat tyres on Miss Paxton's car which was parked by the river.'

'Never seen it,' said Gary.

'Wasn't us,' said Shaun.

Meredith was standing to one side and their eyes slid over to her belligerently. She'd split on them and they wouldn't forget it, they seemed to be saying.

Joss matched their cool denial with calm insistence. 'You were seen, both of you, so there isn't any point in lying about it, I'm afraid.' He got up and came round the desk, putting a firm but kind hand on each boy's shoulder. 'Do you remember the other evening when we were throwing stones in the pond? Each stone made a circle of waves that spread out and grew bigger and bigger.'

'Yes, I remember,' said Shaun, interest livening his face. 'They never ended.'

'That's right,' said Joss. 'And lies are just the same. If you tell one you have to tell another, and they go on and on with no end to them. So it isn't really worth it, is it, boys?'

Gary still looked sullen, but he shook his head. 'No, Mr Hamblyn.'

Shaun echoed him.

'Now, I think an apology is due to Miss Paxton. She

was all for letting you get away with it, but I can't allow that. You have to learn to respect other people's property. I've rung Ted Northby at the garage and we've agreed that you will wash cars for him until you've earned enough to pay for having those tyres done. Do you reckon that's fair?'

'Reckon so, Mr Hamblyn,' muttered Gary.

'Sorry, Miss Paxton,' said Shaun.

Oh, yes, he was fair where they were concerned. Meredith had to admit it. The boys respected him and didn't argue about their punishment. They probably even looked forward to an hour or two at the garage washing cars.

She studied him. His mouth was set in a hard line, firm and uncompromising, and the square jaw showed the strength of his character. Every problem was dealt with according to its merit and she imagined his mind neatly pigeonholed, with correct answers ready for every situation. But that fairness on which he prided himself did not extend as far as Meredith Paxton. The shadow of Piers was between them, not like the ripples on a pond, but a torrent of emotional antagonism that couldn't easily be checked, and his unbiased judgement was missing. Those shrewd green eyes sent a chill down her spine as they rested on her unexpectedly, sensing her scrutiny, and a prickling of unpleasant premonition filled her with disquiet. She was alone in her dislike of him, and vulnerable, and that little demonstration of fair-mindedness hadn't impressed her as much as he intended.

'I hope that met with your approval,' he said, when the boys had gone. He hadn't like reprimanding them and made her feel the blame was hers for necessitating it.

'You seem anxious that it should,' commented Meredith.

'They're basically good boys, and I want them to learn the right code of behaviour.' His tone had mellowed. 'I also want to apologise for hurting you this morning.'

He was near her, and a faint smell of discreet aftershave drifted over, disturbing her. Her glance settled on his mouth again, watching the easing of it as a half smile appeared, and her own lips began to tingle. To her consternation she felt herself succumbing to a collection of physically arousing symptoms too complicated to assimilate, and a sudden urge to know if that handsome mouth would feel good against hers had to be fiercely quashed. The need to keep her distance with Joss Hamblyn increased rapidly as awareness of his sexual attraction sounded alarm bells in her ears. What on earth was the matter with her? She must have taken leave of her senses!

'Thank you,' was all she said. But she made a mental note to keep a high barrier between herself and Joss, bridged only by impersonal contact at work. It was the only way she could be sure of immunity to the forceful threat of his personality.

May slipped quickly into June and the weather changed. It became cold and wet, as if summer had decided not to come after all, and the path down to the stables at Combe Lodge became waterlogged. Meredith spent a lot of her spare time there converting the loft into a habitable room where she could take a scribbling pad and pencil, for she intended to write Piers's biography while details and events and precious memories of him were still clear in her mind. But before she could start on the project two things happened which put paid to it indefinitely.

The first disruption occurred the second week in June. Meredith's grandmother, who lived in Scotland, suffered a severe heart attack, and as there were no other relatives it meant that Julia Paxton had to go up there and see what she could do for her mother.

'We'll manage just fine,' said Howard. 'Mrs Taylor won't mind putting in more hours, and Meredith and I are quite capable of looking after ourselves.'

Mrs Taylor was the daily help, and quite indispensable.

'Don't worry, darling,' said Meredith, 'I can cope with Daddy. He's as good as gold. And if I need advice I'll phone Ellen.'

She and Ellen had become friends, as Julia had hoped they would, and with the comforting thought that Ellen's practical help would be there if needed it was easy to persuade her mother to catch the first available train.

The second thing that happened had far-reaching consequences, and occurred only a day after Julia had left for Scotland.

Meredith was alone in the office. Joss was attending Court and had already phoned asking her to cancel his afternoon appointments as he wasn't going to be back until late, so when there was a commotion in the outer office she knew it wasn't anyone who was expected. She heard a child shouting, but took no notice, until the door of Joss's room burst open and Ellen was there with Oliver, the baby, in her arms.

'Meredith, they say Joss is out, but I *must* see him. How long will he be, or where can I get hold of him? It's desperately urgent!'

She had never seen Ellen agitated before. The wonderful calmness that usually soothed everyone else had disappeared and she was in a regular flap.

'Sit down a minute, Ellen,' Meredith said gently, guiding her to the armchair in spite of protests. 'Joss won't be back today. He's in Court. Can you tell *me* what's the matter and perhaps I can help.'

'I don't know what to do,' cried Ellen. 'I phoned your mother just now and I can't get any reply. . . .'

'She's in Scotland.'

'Oh, no!' Her wail was imitated by the baby, who thought it was a joke. 'I've had some terrible news, Meredith. Ian has been very badly injured in a bomb blast and I've got to fly out to him straight away. He's been moved to a big military hospital, and if I don't get there within the next twenty-four hours it may be too late.'

'Ellen! I'm *so* sorry.' Meredith put an arm round the other girl as she choked back a sob.

Ellen looked up at her, her eyes swimming with tears. 'But what am I going to do with the children?'

There was a tea stain on her white blouse and her denim skirt had been washed so often the colour was almost non-existent. It was easy to see why when Kirsty came running in and climbed on to her mother's lap, regardless of muddy shoes. With two children now bouncing on her and squealing playfully it was no wonder the poor girl couldn't think straight.

Meredith took a deep breath and put on her most efficient, nothing-is-impossible air which always got results.

'That's the least of your worries,' she said, in a reassuring tone that she hoped was convincing enough to fool herself as well as Ellen. '*I* can manage the children for you. No problem at all.'

CHAPTER FOUR

THE baby was screaming, and Kirsty was tugging at a piece of French bread that Shaun had taken from her, both children shouting with full lung power until even the baskets suspended from the ceiling seemed to squeak in protest. Only Gary was quiet, taking advantage of the changed routine to fill himself with extra bread and jam which Ellen had said was not good for him. Wet wellingtons were scattered in muddy patches over the dark red quarry tiles, and the rush mats were sliding from view under the table along with various toys. Dirty pans filled the sink, and crockery from the eventful high tea was jumbled ready for washing, remnants of the meal which Gary hadn't cared to finish up coagulating on plates with nursery rhyme edges. Meredith left it all while she boiled some milk for Oliver's bottle, feeling the sooner she could get *him* fed, bathed and put to bed the easier it would be to deal with the rest. The kitchen was in chaos, and Ellen had only been gone two hours.

In the midst of all this confusion, Joss came home. Such was the noise that no one heard his car, or the front door, or his footsteps down the hall. When he stood in the kitchen doorway, surveying the scene with growing astonishment, it still took several seconds before his presence was felt; and then all eyes turned towards him.

'What the hell is going on here?' he demanded, his voice deep and reverberating with displeasure. 'Where's Ellen?'

Shaun and Gary scuffed their feet awkwardly, but

Kirsty ran to Joss with a great cry of delight, attaching herself to him by clasping both little arms tightly round his legs.

'Uncle Joss, I'm *so* glad you've come! Mummy's gone away.'

'Ellen is on her way to Saudi Arabia,' said Meredith quietly.

She hoisted the baby higher on to her shoulder, and began transferring the milk from the saucepan to the feeding bottle. Joss was across the kitchen in a few strides. He took the baby from her furiously.

'Don't you know better than to have him that close to the stove! And never pour hot liquid like that while you've got a child in your arms. What are you trying to do? Scald him?'

Oliver continued to scream a moment longer, then his little feet kicked against Joss's chest like an athlete in training and the screams turned to gurgles. Kirsty bobbed up and down beside him, trying to gain attention, but he turned to the two boys near the table.

'Shaun, Gary, start getting some of that washing-up done. You're quite old enough to lend a hand. And you, Kirsty, can stop being a nuisance.' He issued orders as if he was on a parade ground, and the children obeyed him at once. Even Kirsty picked up her boots and stood them tidily near the back door. With everything organised he returned to Meredith. 'Now you can explain what you meant about Ellen.'

The heat from the stove had reddened her face, but his admonitory tone made it burn all the more. She hadn't been home to change her clothes, and the flared black skirt and frilled blouse she had put on that morning looked as if even the dry-cleaners would throw a fit at the sight of them. No wonder Ellen never looked tidy!

'Ian was caught up in a bomb blast,' she said, trying

to keep her voice from rising. 'Ellen was in a dreadful state. It seems she may not arrive in time to see him. It's that bad.'

'Why wasn't I informed?'

'We both tried to contact you and were told you were not available, so I made all the arrangements for her and said I would look after the children.'

'My word!' exclaimed Joss.

Meredith gritted her teeth. 'And what's *that* supposed to mean?'

He looked round the room at the chaos now being brought under limited control, then back to her, raising his thick, dark eyebrows until she felt the full impact of his scornful gaze.

'It means you've got a helluva nerve,' he said. 'You may have been an expert at organising flights in executive jets for business tycoons, but you've no idea how to manage a household, and you don't know a damn thing about handling children, so what right had you to poke your interfering nose in our affairs without consulting anyone?'

'I used my initiative, as I would in any emergency,' snapped Meredith, so angry at his ingratitude she felt like flinging the baby's bottle at him. 'No doubt *you* would check on all the correct procedures before phoning the fire brigade if the house was burning down!'

'You're too clever by half.'

'And *you* are a self-opinionated hypocrite! You're evading the issue. Ellen was much too distressed to organise anything, and if you'd ever loved anyone enough you'd know how it feels. Ian was her priority, so I arranged a flight straight away, then undertook to do what I could to relieve her mind of other worries. My father has taken her to the airport.' She tested the heat of the milk on her arm. 'Now, if you'll give me the baby I'll see to his bottle. I assure you the milk is the right temperature. And I've cooked some dinner for you, in case you haven't had any. It's in the oven.'

At the mention of Howard's name he relaxed a little, and when she had seated herself in a low chair he put Oliver into her arms. He seemed stunned, and she realised it must have been quite a shock for him to arrive home expecting everything to be normal and finding instead that the whole routine had collapsed without warning.

Probably Ellen would have sprung to attention the minute Joss came in. She had been very anxious that the chops were done ready for him, and as Meredith prided herself on her cooking ability it had been no trouble to prepare an appetising meal and pop it in a slow oven. It had been far more time-consuming trying to get baked beans on toast for the children's tea while they were in such a turmoil over Ellen's sudden departure. They hadn't been in the least co-operative; in fact Shaun and Gary had been deliberately obstructive, waking the baby early so that he howled all through tea, tormenting Kirsty, then falling out with each other. She hadn't shouted at them, much as she had been tempted. It was their way of reacting to unexpected change and they had to be given time to adjust. But her nerves were badly frayed, and Joss's unwarranted attack had provoked a far more heated response than she would have dared to give otherwise.

She settled Oliver in the crook of her arm, his downy head nestling against the wilted frills of her blouse, and gave him the bottle. There was something enchanting about the effect it had on her as she watched him sucking noisily. The warm kitchen became comfortingly serene, in spite of the clatter the boys were making at the sink, and she gradually absorbed the unfamiliar homeliness. Her index finger caressed the baby's head, and when Kirsty crept up to her she drew her close, including her in the automatic urge to show affection, as if they were her children. It was the first time she had experienced the maternal instinct, and if anyone had told her she would find it a heady sensation she would have laughed.

'I'd better phone Mrs Burns and see if she can come back here tonight,' said Joss. Mrs Burns was an elderly widow who came every morning to help Ellen with the children and the housework. 'I presume you haven't thought that far ahead.'

'She's visiting her sister, I'm afraid,' said Meredith, without looking up.

Joss had perched himself on the edge of the table and was staring at her thoughtfully. She could feel the intensity of his gaze, and smiled inwardly, conscious that she was winning a small victory, which didn't please him at all. Had she looked up she would have been surprised to see the true expression in his eyes. They were clouded with bewilderment, and encompassed the whole domestic scene with a wistfulness she would have found very puzzling.

'In that case,' he said, 'I'm sure you've made alternative arrangements. May I know what they are?'

'I shall be staying here myself,' said Meredith.

He left the table and stood in front of her, a lock of hair falling over his forehead. 'You will do no such thing.'

'Why not?'

'I want her to stay,' said Kirsty, pressing her little body closer.

Gary was splashing Shaun, taking advantage of everyone's preoccupation, but he stopped long enough to give his opinion. 'I don't,' he said. 'She's too bossy.'

Joss went over to the sink and emptied the bowl of water, handing the boys a towel to wipe up; then he came back to Meredith, stripping off his jacket and rolling up his sleeves as if he was about to evict her forcibly.

'I'm perfectly capable of seeing to the children myself,' he said. 'I appreciate what you've done, and I'm sure that offer was meant with the best of intentions, but I don't have to tell you it would be hardly the thing for you to spend the night under this roof with Ellen away.'

'And whose reputation are you worried about? Yours or mine?'

Meredith lifted the baby against her shoulder and got to her feet. She faced Joss squarely, her temperature rising.

'Does that matter?' he asked.

'Not particularly, but it would be nice to know. You once said I was more than a secretary to Piers, implying that we slept together, so I'm sure it isn't *my* reputation you think would be harmed. It must be your professional image. In which case I'll leave you to put the baby to bed, and I'll be on my way.'

She held Oliver out to him with both arms, but he didn't take him. Oliver wriggled furiously at having his supper time so disrupted and she had to cuddle him again before he started to cry.

'I don't want Meredith to go,' whimpered Kirsty, clinging to Meredith's skirt.

It was like a marital quarrel. The extraordinary thing was, Meredith was beginning to enjoy it. Feuding with Joss was strangely exciting, and the sparks that flew between them made her skin tingle in a way she didn't attempt to analyse.

'If you must know, it's your father who concerns me most,' he told her. 'I should hate him to be disillusioned about you.'

'My father trusts me completely.'

'You mean he actually believes your relationship with Piers was quite innocent?'

Her eyes hardened. 'I mean he knows *you* are the last person in the world I'd share a bed with!'

'And I assure you I have no intention of taking up where Piers Loring left off,' snarled Joss. 'I don't want any favours.'

It was the cruellest thing he could have said, and there was no longer even an oblique pleasure in sparring with him. They were fighting in earnest. Gary had come up to them and his small blue eyes fixed on them knowingly as he listened.

'You sound like me mum and dad,' Gary observed. 'They used to row like that before me dad walked out.'

Meredith had been about to make a cutting retaliation, but the boy's words brought her up sharply and she was appalled to realise how dreadful their quarrelling must sound to the children. Kirsty had disappeared under the table, and Shaun was gaping at them with much the same expression as Gary. Without saying anything else she put the baby in the carry-cot, steeling herself against his instant wail, and tried not to let Joss see how much he had hurt her. He had turned his back, so she didn't see that there was pain in his eyes, too.

'I'll see you at the office tomorrow morning,' she said, collecting her bag and slipping on her jacket. 'I trust you won't be late. You have an appointment at nine-thirty with Mrs Galmain and she wouldn't approve of being kept waiting.'

She had opened the front door when he called,

'Meredith, wait! You can't rush off like that!'

He was standing in the hallway, his shirt pulled open at the neck, and there was something about him that made her heart contract without warning. She lifted her chin proudly, but let her eyes dwell on him a moment, assessing the strength of his muscular arms and powerful shoulders. It wasn't fair that such an impossible man should be so physically attractive.

'If you're begging me to stay you're wasting your time,' she called back. 'You said you were capable of looking after everything, so I wish you luck. Goodbye, Joss.'

She drove back to Combe Lodge erratically, hoping the local police were nowhere around or they would think she had been drinking. Anger made her movements jerky and she was too overwrought to think clearly. He was an insensitive, callous brute, so full of his own importance he couldn't see farther than the end of his aristocratic nose, and she wished she need never see him again. No sooner did she feel they were beginning to get on better than he let fly again with words like barbed darts. She detested him!

Her father wouldn't be back for a long time yet, so she had the house to herself, and after a while the quietness began to revive her flagged spirits. She even managed to smile ruefully at her damp, bedraggled reflection in the bathroom mirror. There was no make-up left on her face, her hair was like a haystack, and there were crumbs on the front of her crumpled blouse; all this after a couple of hours' domesticity! Never again would she say it was an easy job looking after children. She would rather sit down to a pile of accounts or type out a dozen legal documents any day; it wasn't half so exhausting. She discarded her clothes and stepped thankfully under the shower, revelling in the freshness of hot water cascading over her body.

Why was it, then, that as soon as she sat down to relax with a compelling new novel she found she was unable to concentrate? The quietness all around wasn't restful after all. It had an empty, colourless quality, as if she was sitting in a vacuum, and she found herself thinking of the atmosphere at Eden Farm. It absorbed noise and disruption as if it was part of its heritage, and gave back a feeling of calm that touched the soul with a special magic in spite of everything.

And Joss Hamblyn? She pictured him struggling with children and chores, his irascible manner somehow achieving incredible results. It was silly to hope he would have to pocket his pride and shout for help. He was far too capable, and probably by now the place was as shipshape as it had ever been, the chaos swept away with abrupt orders that the children obeyed and even found amusing. There had to be a core of disguised benevolence in him that she didn't understand and had never been privileged to see.

She couldn't stop thinking about him. The book fell to the floor, and she relived that fierce quarrel that was an extension of all their other antagonistic encounters. How would it end? She couldn't be near him without being aroused by his masculinity, but that arousal brought no pleasure with it; only a desire to run as far as she could before she was caught up in emotions too potent for her to fight against. Their aversion to each other almost made normal conversation impossible, and she could see no way to alter the situation. The fact that her body reacted with such agitation when he was near was a trick of chemistry over which she had no control, and she attributed it to her mental antipathy towards him which was causing peculiar side effects. It would be self-betrayal to reason otherwise. Piers had never caused her unrest like this, even when he let her down and broke promises. She had taken it all in her stride and made allowances for him. So why couldn't she just banish all thoughts of Joss from her mind when she didn't have to be in his company? It wasn't worth letting him monopolise her time like this when there were far more important things to think about.

She couldn't sit still any longer in the silent room. The walls were closing in on her and shadows moved across the carpet eerily as the sun got lower. Feeling the need for air to clear her head, she decided to go down to the stables for a while. A sure way to rid herself of Joss's influence would be to make a real start on her notes about Piers, and she felt immediately cheered by the prospect.

The rain had left enormous puddles across the path and she jumped over them, her hair bouncing in a youthful ponytail behind her as it had done when she was a little girl, and as always she began to feel her troubles were being left behind in the house. Wet bushes trailed against the sleeves of her blue sweat shirt and the white pants she had changed into quickly became mud-spattered, but she sang to herself, letting the tranquillity of the June evening dispel her problems until tomorrow.

Had she known more trouble awaited her in the stables, she might not have been so lighthearted.

The door was ajar. Meredith paused, lifting her head suspiciously, because she never came away without locking it, and as far as she knew she had the only key. She opened it another inch, cautiously so that the hinges didn't creak, and listened. For a moment she heard nothing; then a bird flew up into the rafters, making her nerves tighten, and she looked up to try and see what had frightened it. The ladder up to the hay loft was in place and there was no other movement, so she crept stealthily inside, her heart beating like a steam hammer. If it was a vagrant sleeping rough she would have to inform the police.

Wet weather had made the old timbers smell strongly of wood rot and resin, and as she took a deep breath it filled her nostrils. But there was another smell she couldn't identify, convincing her that someone was there, and she had the choice of either going back to the house to phone the police, or to challenge the intruder and find out who it was first. Surely in Edencombe there couldn't be any great danger. She went to the foot of the ladder and called, her foot on the first rung ready to tip it away and cut off the only means of retreat if necessary.

'I know there's someone there. You're trespassing. Will you please leave before I have to get the police?'

Not a sound. Then just as she was about to climb up and investigate there was a scuffle behind her, and two small figures darted so swiftly to the door she scarcely had time to look round. But she recognised them. Oh, yes, she had seen them do a disappearing act before after making mischief.

She ran to the door and hauled it open wide. 'Gary! Shaun! Come back here this minute!' she shouted.

It would have been amazing if they had taken any notice of her. They merged into the twilight shadows with hardly any noise, and the only thing she caught sight of was Gary's fair bullet head before they hid themselves completely. Guessing they would wait until she had gone back inside the stables, she stayed by the door for several seconds, conscious of their wary eyes on her somewhere out there, like foxes peering out of a lair. And she smiled to herself. So the mighty Joss Hamblyn was not infallible after all. His charges had escaped into the night rather than go to bed, fooling him the moment his back was turned.

She knew she would have to go after them. Two small London boys shouldn't be out alone after dark, wandering the countryside. Apart from perhaps coming to harm themselves, she had the distinct feeling they wouldn't have too much respect for other local property. She could already see that the stable lock had been picked.

She waited about a minute before making a show of going back, drawing the door to as she went, but she only stood to one side and could still see the place where they had hidden. She wished she had worn something dark and hoped the white pants weren't visible in the dimness, because the boys were cute as monkeys and knew every trick. Even now they could have slipped away through the bushes, though it wouldn't be easy to get through the garden undetected. No, she felt sure they would bide their time and then make a getaway along the path which led up to the moors. Sure enough, a few minutes later she heard the branches rustle and the two youngsters made a dash for the gate.

They were much quicker than Meredith. She gave chase immediately, calling their names, but they were nimble as goats and had climbed over the gate and away before she could get near them. The path was rough and steep, too muddy for her to gain any speed, and she had to run up the side of it, scratching her feet on the heather roots. She could see them ahead of her, running full pelt on to the open moor with no thought as to where they were heading. How far would they go? She daren't let them out of her sight because the light was fading and the moors were dangerous to anyone not familiar with them, the waterlogged ground treacherous underfoot.

She wondered whether Joss had missed them yet, and if so what he was doing about it. He wouldn't be able to go far from the house and leave the other children alone there. He would be absolutely furious! Well, it served him right for being so beastly; and for being too proud to accept any help.

The boys had disappeared. She was on top of the ridge and she couldn't see them anywhere. Moorland stretched away as far as the eye could see, the remnants of sunset colours staining the sky burnt orange and amber on the horizon, but the deep folds of gorse-covered land were being shrouded in shadow now, and she began to get nervous. She had known the moors all her life, but once it got dark it was very easy to lose all sense of direction, and she had heard of people walking round in circles all night. Whatever happened she couldn't let those children get lost. They didn't have warm clothing on for one thing, and even in June the night air could get pretty cold. She kept on calling them until her voice was hoarse.

Suddenly there was a scream way ahead of her, followed by several more, and she heard Gary shouting. The bracken and gorse impeded her, but she stumbled towards the cries as fast as she could, guessing already what she would find. There were bogs on this part of the moor, and the heavy rain would increase the danger of getting caught in one. There was a pain in her chest from rushing, but she didn't stop until she came to the two terrified boys.

'It's Shaun, miss!' Gary cried, his voice rising hysterically. 'He's sinking in the mud and I can't get him out!'

'Stay perfectly still, Shaun. Don't move at all!' Meredith shouted. The boy was up to his thighs in mud, and the more he struggled the worse it became. She grabbed Gary's arm and pointed to a stunted tree over to the right. 'Help me get the thickest branch we can carry.'

Shaun was crying pitifully when they got back, but he had obeyed her and was no deeper in the bog.

'It was sensible of you not to try and get near him, Gary, or you would have been in there as well,' she said, making her voice light to reassure them. 'Hang on, Shaun, we'll have you out of there any minute now.'

The branch they had got was strong enough for the purpose and not too heavy to sink. With Gary's help she managed to slide it over the mud until Shaun was able to reach out and catch hold, then she called instructions to him calmly, and with a bit of hard pulling his little legs gradually came clear. Only when he was safe on firm ground again did she realise how much she was trembling. Still on her knees in the mud, she clasped both boys to her, hugging them thankfully.

'Good job you came, miss,' said Gary gruffly, and she knew it was his awkward way of saying thanks. But Shaun put his thin little arms round her neck and she felt his tear-stained face against her cheek as another squall of heavy rain descended upon them.

It was dark when they got back to Eden Farm. The bedraggled trio went round to the back of the house and Meredith opened the kitchen door, calling for Joss. He came through from the lounge, his hair dishevelled as if he'd been raking his fingers through it, and when he saw her his face was a mixture of fury and relief.

'I knew damned well *you'd* be at the bottom of this!' he raged. She might have guessed anger would be foremost. 'I don't know what your motive was in taking the boys off with you, but it was irresponsible to say the least, and I'm bloody mad! I was on the point of ringing the police.'

'We were having a game and rather lost ourselves,' said Meredith, biting back a more cutting retort.

'And what sort of state do you call this to come back in? I've never seen anything so disgraceful! It's a good job Ellen isn't here. You'd better get those clothes off and cleaned up quickly.'

'Just who do you think you're talking to?' she demanded.

'A girl old enough to know better. You've not got as much sense as Kirsty! Even she knows she'd be in real trouble if she came in soaking wet and filthy dirty.'

He was eyeing her incredulously and she realised just what a mess she must look. The white pants were saturated and covered in mud, clinging uncomfortably to her thighs; her sweat shirt, equally wet and clinging, had moulded itself to her body, and her hair hung round her face and shoulders like strands of seaweed. Both she and the boys were already making puddles on the floor where they stood.

'Shaun, Gary, go on up to the bathroom and get in a hot bath straight away,' she said, giving each a reassuring squeeze. 'Everything'll be all right.'

'Like hell it will!' stormed Joss. His shirt had come open to the waist and beads of perspiration clung to the mass of black hair on his chest. He obviously hadn't been having too easy a time of it, and she rejoiced at the evidence. His eyes bored into her, hooded and unreadable. 'Okay, you boys, do as she says. But *you*, Meredith, are going to give me an explanation and an apology.'

Shaun and Gary took the opportunity of escape the second it was offered, but it was Gary who pulled up abruptly just as he was about to skid round the door after the younger boy. He turned and came back, hanging his head and clasping his pudgy hands behind him.

'Mr Hamblyn, it wasn't Meredith's fault,' he said sheepishly. 'Me and Shaun, we thought it would be a lark to stay out late with Aunt Ellen away, and we were in that old barn place of Mr Paxton's when she saw us. We thought she'd be mad, so we ran off up the hill, and then Shaun got stuck in the mud and she came and hauled him out. Please don't be mad at her.'

Joss frowned, and there was a significant pause. Then: 'Is this true?' he asked Meredith.

A smile flickered across her lips. 'It was you who taught them it's simpler to tell the truth,' she said. 'You should be proud they took notice of you.'

He looked round at the boy and a gradual thaw took place, not so as to be dazzlingly noticeable, but at least the atmosphere became less cold.

'Thank you, Gary,' he said. 'We'll talk about it in the morning, but you did the right thing. Now run off upstairs.' He started to follow him, saying to Meredith: 'Stay there while I get a skirt and top of Ellen's for you.'

Standing near the Aga where it was warm, Meredith found a towel and began rubbing her hair. With her head bent and her back to the door, she didn't hear Joss return a few minutes later, so when he touched her shoulder she jerked upright and almost overbalanced. He caught her arms and she felt herself drawn back against him, his chin resting lightly on the top of her head.

'I'm the one who must apologise,' he said, the low, rich voice full of contrition. 'As usual you had great presence of mind and I ought to have known better than to blow my top. With everyone else I think first and speak afterwards, but for some reason with you it's always the other way round. I'm sorry.'

It must have made her dizzy hanging her head down. Her heart was beating crazily and where her back rested against his chest it seemed as if there was a patch of fire. A warmth spread through her, pounding in her ears as it surged upwards, and she twisted away from him in alarm.

'It doesn't matter,' she said, facing him. She made herself take a long, slow breath and hoped the dirt would disguise the colour that flooded her cheeks.

Joss held out a cotton wrap-round skirt and a cheesecloth blouse. 'Take off those wet things before you get chilled. And as soon as the boys have finished in the bathroom I suggest you take a shower.'

'It offends you to see me untidy, doesn't it?'

She took the clothes, remembering how a previous argument had stemmed from much the same source. But this time amusement crept into his eyes and a half smile lifted the corners of his mouth.

'On the contrary, I find the sight of you in a dishevelled state so much more disturbing than the prim image you present daily at the office, I can't trust myself to keep my hands off you.'

Meredith gasped and moved swiftly across the kitchen, peeled off the wet sweat-shirt and slipped her arms into Ellen's blouse as quickly as she could. But before she could button it he was near her again.

'Stay away from me, Joss,' she warned. A constriction in her throat made her voice sound hoarse, and the air around them was charged with an emotional current so strong she crouched back, finding herself against the wall. He said nothing, but the magnetism of his green eyes attracted her forcefully and she found herself staring into them with unblinking fascination as she flattened her back against the tiled wall. He towered over her, unnerving in his very nearness, and she was more sexually aware of him than she had been of any man. As he took hold of her, her body arched towards him. His mouth hovered above hers just long enough to bring an attempted protest, but every heartbeat increased her response to him and her cries were lost in a kiss that left her weak and aching.

His hands caressed her back beneath the flimsy cotton blouse, and rivers of ecstasy flowed through her. She had never known that such exquisite sensation existed, and for a few moments she abandoned herself to it, forgetting even whose arms and lips were creating this havoc within her. She responded to the increasing pressure of his lips, but when his hand slipped round to touch her breast she was suddenly awakened to the madness in which they indulged, and she dragged herself away from him, hardly able to breathe.

'For Pete's sake, Joss, leave me alone!' she gasped, clutching the blouse across the front of her. 'I don't want you near me!'

His hands fell to his sides. 'You could have fooled me,' he drawled. 'If that's the way you reacted to Piers Loring he was a very lucky guy.'

'Piers would never have taken advantage of a situation like this. He was far too considerate. You had no business touching me!'

'Maybe not. But you can't deny you enjoyed it.' There was a fire in his eyes, smouldering green fire that held mystic enchantment, urging her to return to his arms. She needed all her strength to resist him.

'I hated it! I don't want you near me again!' she cried, regardless of whether it was the truth.

'We'll see,' said Joss.

He shrugged his shoulders as if it was a joke, and a smile broadened his mouth. He raised one eyebrow questioningly and if there had been anything handy Meredith would have thrown it at him. As it was she picked up her sweat-shirt and flounced away from him, determined to maintain a semblance of decent behaviour. A show of temper would only provoke him more.

'I hope you have a quiet night with the children,' she said. 'Goodnight!'

The phone rang just as she was leaving. She had reached the kitchen door when it shrilled into life, and thinking it might be news of Ellen she paused while Joss answered it. He went into the lounge and she couldn't hear what he was saying, but she could tell by the tone of his voice it was nothing personal, so she started off down the hall, only to be called back.

'Meredith, wait!' A minute later he came out to her, all sign of his previous mood gone. 'That was the police,' he said, and seeing her startled expression, hastened to reassure her. 'It's all right, nothing's wrong. At least not for us, except that I've got to go out and I don't know how long I shall have to be. It appears Sid

Frank's son has killed his wife and they've taken him into custody, but he refuses to say anything without his solicitor present. The police would rather it was now.'

'Oh, Joss, how awful!' She knew there had been a lot of correspondence about the Frank boy's matrimonial problems, but she hadn't realised they had reached such terrible proportions.

'I know it's an imposition,' he went on, 'especially after what happened, but do you think you could possibly stay here after all? I can't leave the children alone.'

What choice did she have? She hesitated long enough for him to know she was not jumping at the idea, then she inclined her head slowly.

'As there's no alternative it seems I'll have to,' she said. 'I take it I can use Ellen's bedroom.'

The worried frown he had worn since coming back from the phone eased away. 'Thanks, Meredith. I promise I'll be as quick as I can.'

She stood very straight. 'You don't need to hurry. I don't want to see anything more of you tonight!'

CHAPTER FIVE

THE house was eerily quiet. Meredith had come upstairs to check that the children were all asleep, and now she was wondering which was Ellen's bedroom. She had thought Joss might not be long and she would be able to go home, but the time was getting on for midnight and he hadn't returned.

She stood on the apple-green carpeted landing and looked at the white doors with their enamelled finger plates, trying to decide which to open first. She had been into the nursery where Oliver and Kirsty were sleeping soundly, and knew which room Gary and Shaun occupied, so it left a choice of four more doors. She tried the one nearest her, and found it was Joss's. She was about to close it again hurriedly, but an overpowering curiosity consumed her and she went inside.

It was a very masculine room, the oak beams left their natural colour, giving a sombre effect which was relieved by cream walls and a cream quilted bedcover. Wood panelling behind the bed gleamed darkly and an arrangement of country prints hung above an antique wash-stand which was purely decorative as there was an adjoining bathroom to the master suite, the door to it ajar over to the left.

It wasn't a particularly tidy room. Joss's love of books was evident in the number scattered around, and the suit he had worn at the office all day was carelessly draped over a chair. Meredith went over to it, picked up the jacket and straightened the sleeves. The feel of it beneath her fingers was peculiarly stirring, as if his

vibrant personality had imparted separate life into
the fine cloth, and she could imagine it was still warm
from contact with him. Her heart, which had taken
such a time to quieten after he left, jerked back to the
irregular thumping, hammering against her ribs, and
the strength sapped from her legs. She flung the jacket
down.

Whatever was the matter with her? She wasn't afraid
of Joss Hamblyn. On the contrary, it gave her great
satisfaction to oppose him when she felt she was in the
right, and their battles livened things up considerably.
With Piers, satisfaction had lain in their ability to work
together so well, minds attuned, but she found working
with Joss a never-ending attempt to prevent conflict. It
wasn't anything to do with the work itself. She had
adapted quickly to the routine of a solicitor's office and
enjoyed the challenge it had offered. No, it was Joss
himself. He hadn't fully accepted her, wasn't prepared
to forget about Piers, and kept up a cruel sarcasm
about anything concerning him which she couldn't
understand. No matter how hard she tried she just
couldn't like Joss.

But like him or not, nothing could stop the way
she reacted to his physical attraction. She groaned,
remembering the shameless way she had pressed herself
against him and how the first touch of his lips on hers
had sent a pulsating current coursing through her veins.
There was no answer to the mysterious question of
sexual chemistry. The last thing she wanted was to be
guided by a craving for sensation, and she determined
never to be swayed again by that powerful male
magnetism.

All the same, she was drawn towards the bed and
stood beside it, bewildered by the complexity of her
emotions. She'd never thought it possible to be so
disturbed by an inanimate object, but the place where

Joss Hamblyn lay down to sleep each night had a
mesmerising effect on her and she trailed her glance
slowly upwards from the foot to the head, returning to
the pillows where his head would rest. She brushed the
back of her hand over the top pillow, closing her eyes;
then snatched it away, chiding herself for being so
ridiculously sensuous. There was something about his
room that played wicked tricks with her reasoning.

But her curiosity was still not appeased. Treading
softly on the thick, ochre-coloured carpet, she went into
the bathroom where his personal possessions were even
more intimate. She had the strangest feeling that if she
found out details about him like what kind of
toothpaste he used and what soap he liked she would be
better equipped to deal with him. Nonsense, of course,
but it gave her a little more insight into the type of man
he was. She picked up a bottle of after-shave,
recognising the spicy smell, and an involuntary quiver
went through her. It made him seem so near she even
glanced over her shoulder guiltily before laughing at
herself. This really was quite ridiculous! Only people
who were madly infatuated behaved in this silly,
childish fashion.

She froze to the spot. The little ante-room, so
intrinsically belonging to Joss, came alive with
reminders of him, permeating her senses, drugging her.
She couldn't really be infatuated with the man; the very
thought made her protest aloud. Yet what was she
doing here, touching things that belonged to him with
all the wishful longing of someone who craved to touch
the man himself?

'The word for it is lust,' she told herself disgustedly.
It was the only word that could describe her present
feelings, and she repeated it so that the implications
wouldn't be lost. It was quite wrong to let purely
physical demands take over when there was absolutely

nothing about him that endeared itself to her, and if she valued her self-respect she had to put a stop to such ideas straight away.

She was just replacing the bottle of after-shave on the shelf when she heard the car come up the drive and pull up outside the front door. If Joss found her here there was no knowing what interpretation he would put on it. With rising panic Meredith hurried out on to the landing and closed the door behind her.

Almost at once the door bell rang. He must have forgotten his key. She waited a second, her heart pounding, before going warily down the stairs. She didn't want to see him again tonight, especially now after the revelation that had dawned on her so unexpectedly.

The bell rang again. It was past midnight and she was alone in the house in charge of four small children. Supposing it wasn't Joss? Her time in London had taught her never to open the door to anyone late at night unless you were absolutely certain who it was; but this was Edencombe. She went to the door and opened it a fraction.

'It's all right, Meredith, it's me,' said her father.

'Daddy!' she cried, in pleased surprise. 'Come on in.'

'I just got back home and you weren't there. I guessed this was where you'd be, but I thought I'd better have a word with Joss and see that everything's okay. Where is he?'

'He's out,' she said, leading Howard through to the kitchen. 'He had a call from the police about Sid Frank's son, so I had to stay with the children. Did Ellen get off all right?'

'She did. Very apprehensive about Ian and worried about the children, but I assured her they were all in good hands. Tell me about Sid Frank.'

Meredith made coffee and related all she knew,

discussing the case with her father at some length while they drank it, but she was listening all the time for Joss to return. Her mind was preoccupied and in the middle of the conversation she found herself blurting out the most unexpected question.

'Daddy, why did Joss hate Piers so much?'

Howard put down his coffee cup and leaned back in the chair. It wasn't fair to shoot such a question at him when he wasn't ready for it, but he only deliberated for a few seconds. He stroked his elegant chin, and his acutely perceptive eyes rested on her thoughtfully.

'It's quite a long story, Meredith, and knowing your loyalty to the Loring family I'm not sure whether you want to hear it,' he said.

She had a stab of foreboding, but was adamant. 'If I didn't, I wouldn't have asked.'

He still looked dubious. She was wearing Ellen's skirt and blouse and it was clear the evening must have been eventful by the way she seemed unaware of her untidy appearance. Meredith was always meticulously tidy. He didn't embarrass her by asking what had happened.

'It's all to do with Corinne Loring,' he said, watching her expression. 'You see, before she married Mac everyone thought Joss was the one she would choose, although I didn't know either of them then. Apparently they were always together and Joss idolised her. But I imagine Mac Loring dangled his wealth in front of her nose and she couldn't resist it. He's rather good at giving the impression that he's got plenty of money.'

Meredith interrupted him. 'Just the facts, Daddy, please. I don't want your opinions.'

'I'm sorry, but you see Corinne was taken in by him just as your mother was years ago. It was just before you met Piers, and I suppose Mac was comfortably solvent and between bankruptcies at the time, but even then it didn't take Corinne long to discover Piers was the apple of his father's eye and anything he asked for his father would give him. That was all very well until he hatched up the idea of going into big business without a penny to his name. It didn't please me when I knew *you* were prepared to help finance him, but I'd no power to stop you and all I could offer was advice. Mac sank all his money in it, then embezzled the little Corinne had and sold her jewellery without her knowledge. It was despicable. Worse than that. . . .'

'So I suppose Corinne blamed Piers for the break-up of her marriage and Joss hated Piers for hurting his beloved Corinne.'

'That's roughly it,' Howard agreed. 'Corinne sought Joss for legal advice and the divorce went through on the grounds of irretrievable breakdown. Joss squeezed every penny he could out of Mac and did very well for her, but he can't forgive the Lorings for what they did.'

Meredith was silent, digesting the information thoughtfully. She had only met Corinne a few times, and then only socially, so they had never said much to each other, but she could remember feeling that Mac had taken on more than he bargained for when he married her. Oh, she was a very beautiful girl. Men couldn't keep their eyes off her, and she played up to them all the time, knowing her beauty and bubbling personality were irresistible, but underneath all that charm there was stone; no heart at all, Meredith was sure. She also knew quite well that Corinne had tried to capture Piers as well, and had become vindictive when she failed. Piers had had no time for her. But Joss was so susceptible he couldn't see farther than that lovely exterior, and he had gone on fighting her battles for her even after she had betrayed him and married someone else. Meredith gave an astonished little laugh. He was a much bigger fool than she had thought he was.

'I suppose Joss now hopes to get back on the same footing with her as he was before Mac appeared on the scene,' she said.

'Corinne means a lot to him,' said Howard. 'He certainly never seems to have been interested in any other woman. Yes, I imagine one day they will probably marry, if he can persuade her.'

There was a strange, tight feeling in her chest. It angered her that any man could be so stupid, and she began to wish she hadn't been so eager to find out his reasons for things. She looked round her with enlightenment. He must have furnished this beautiful house for Corinne, ready for when she condescended to be his wife. What a terrible waste! The picture of her at Eden Farm didn't fit somehow, and Meredith hoped she would never have to see her come down here and take possession. The thought of it made her feel quite sick, because Corinne would destroy all the homeliness, all the enveloping warmth that greeted friends and strangers alike, and she would fill it with her brittle acquaintances who sponged on anyone with facilities for a good time. There would be no lovely family atmosphere with Corinne around.

Yet even as she unhappily contemplated the change Meredith surprised herself. She had never been particularly drawn towards a close family life. Being an only one, she had been a rather solitary child and had never known what it was like to be part of a muddled, happy household where tidiness was least important. It must be some of Ellen's motherly personality rubbing off on her.

Her father was giving her an oddly quizzical smile.

'You don't like the idea of Joss and Corinne marrying, do you?' he said, reading her thoughts.

She considered her reply. Then: 'No, not really. She would take over this place and change it beyond recognition, and then what would Ellen and the children do?'

'They can't stay here for ever. Ellen's already on the lookout for property somewhere near so that she can set up a home of her own as soon as Ian comes home. Pray God he will.' Howard frowned momentarily at the uncertain prospect. 'And you must admit this house is far too big for Joss to live in on his own.'

'It needs to be filled with children,' said Meredith.

'It needs a wife first,' smiled Howard. 'But talking of children, I was on the phone to your mother this morning and she's sitting up there in Scotland dreaming up ambitious plans to get started on the holiday home for deprived youngsters that she and Ellen are so keen on. She intends to get a fund registered and start raising money as soon as she gets back. She told me to tell you a big barbecue in our garden is the first item on the agenda and can you start thinking about it.'

'A barbecue!'

'She said it sounded more exciting than the usual fête.'

Meredith laughed. 'Trust Mummy! Though I must say it could be fun.'

Howard was just looking at his watch and checking it with the clock as he had a habit of doing, when there was the sound of Joss's car drawing up on the gravel drive. It coincided with a cry from upstairs, indicating that Oliver was awake. Of all the untimely things to happen!

She met Joss at the door as she was on her way up to the baby. He looked tired, his eyes drawn and distant so that when they lighted on her it was almost as if he had forgotten that she would be at the house and not Ellen. Meredith hesitated, a wave of compassion sweeping over her so unexpectedly she could have gone up to him with a sympathetic touch, for all the world like a woman who had waited up for her husband. She stopped herself in time. Whatever had possessed her!

'My father's in the kitchen,' she said. 'Perhaps he'll make you some coffee while I see to the baby.'

She even sounded like a wife! She couldn't remember ever having a similar sympathy for Piers when he was overworked and too exhausted to do anything but flop into the chair in her flat and stay there a whole evening.

And it was wasted on Joss.

'A stiff whisky would be more appropriate,' he said. 'And as soon as I've had a few words with Howard I need some sleep, so I hope Oliver isn't going to have one of his more fractious nights.'

'Do they happen often?' she asked anxiously.

'About once a week, and we're due for one any time,' he said, stalking off to the kitchen.

Oh, dear. Meredith's heart sank. She went up to the nursery fleet-footed, her mind only on pacifying Oliver as quickly as possible. He had kicked off his covers and was yelling lustily by the time she got to him and she snatched him out of the cot, hoping he was not old enough to be missing his mother already. It was a wonder he hadn't wakened Kirsty as well, but she was still sleeping peacefully, obviously used to nocturnal disturbances and able to ignore them.

There were facilities for heating up a bottle in one corner of the room, and this she did before sitting down with Oliver in the low, armless chair. She didn't know whether it was time for him to be fed or not, but it seemed the most likely way of stopping him making a noise, and to her relief it worked. The only thing was she hadn't realised what a long, tedious job it could be, and she began to feel very drowsy. She hadn't realised either how tired she was herself. Surely she couldn't have dozed off, and yet she didn't hear Joss come up the stairs. The next thing she knew he was bending over her, taking the baby from her as the bottle fell to the floor.

'It's been quite a day,' he said softly, cradling the little boy in his strong arms, and carrying him over to the cot. 'You're not used to it, Meredith.'

When his voice was low and soft like that she found it the most stirring sound in the world. It never failed to affect her, and this time she didn't try to find any ulterior reason why her limbs went weak.

For a moment or two Oliver gurgled and threatened to stay awake.

'I don't suppose you thought to change him, did you,' said Joss, with a return to the old impatience. Then he proceeded to do it himself while she watched, marvelling at his capability.

'Now perhaps we can all get some rest,' he went on, when the job was done and the baby in the cot closed his eyes without another murmur. He drew Meredith outside, and steered her towards the door on the landing immediately opposite his own. 'Your father didn't wait for you. I got one of Ellen's nighties out for you and put it on the bed. This is her room.'

He opened the door and stood aside for her to pass. He was so brusque she knew he couldn't wait to get away from her and seek the privacy of his own bedroom where he needn't be bothered any more with her irritating presence.

'Thank you, Joss,' was all she said. She had an equal need for escape.

But once she was alone, strange, alien thoughts came crowding back. The conversation with her father tormented her, bringing unwanted pictures of Joss with Corinne Loring. She couldn't understand herself for being so disturbed by them. In many ways they deserved each other, and no doubt Joss would be feeling far from tired right now if Corinne was in the house. *She* wouldn't have meekly closed the bedroom door and let him disappear either. But then Corinne had a strong liking for Joss Hamblyn, which was reciprocated, whereas Meredith had no patience with him whatsoever, and the only strong feelings she had were aversion. She had learned a lot tonight.

Ellen's room was beautiful, bearing the stamp of her artistry, and when Meredith switched on the lamp beside the bed she began to feel soothed. From the curtains of peach velvet to the peach rosebud wallpaper there was an aura of warmth, and she soaked up the atmosphere thankfully. It had been a very long day. There was a shower unit in one corner where she freshened up before slipping into the homely cotton nightdress that lay waiting on the bed. It ought then to have been easy to drop straight off to sleep, but somehow her mind was still much too active and she found herself listening: was it for sounds from the nursery, or for movement in Joss's room? To her annoyance she was acutely conscious of how near he was.

For a long time she lay very still in the unfamiliar bed, trying to banish every thought of Joss from her head. She purposely dwelt on Piers, something she had not done since his death, for even when memories crowded in on her unbidden she always found them too painful. But tonight it was a relief to think of him, a comfort. If they'd been married that fateful morning instead of him dashing off to Paris, what would her life have been like now? So uncertain were their plans they hadn't even decided on a permanent place to live and would no doubt have made do with her flat until Piers could find time to spare for personal matters. Heaven alone knew when that would have been. She would probably have had to arrange everything herself, just as she had done the wedding plans. And as she thought about it deeply she uncovered the uncomfortable truth that she had always done all the running. Piers had never talked of marriage except when she had forced the subject on him.

The room was getting unbearably stuffy. She got up and drew back the velvet curtains, letting in a beam of moonlight that illuminated a mirror opposite and showed her another picture of herself. In the plain, unglamorous nightie, her hair loose about her shoulders, she looked very young and ordinary, not a bit like the sophisticated girl Piers had enjoyed putting on display as if she was an expensive acquisition. She hadn't wanted all the valuable presents he had showered on her, but when she protested he had joked about her being a decorative showcase for his new-found wealth and they had laughed about it together. But just how long would it have taken for her to grow tired of being just another of Piers's assets? Because that was all she had been. The revelation came to her in the same instant that she knew there was far more to be had out of life. She wanted rewarding things, like a home, a baby to cuddle, and a loving husband, and she would have had none of these with Piers. Though it hurt her pride to do so, she had to admit that Joss had been right after all, because it was possible that she had had a lucky escape.

She pushed the window open wide, breathing in the clear night air that did wonders for her spirits, then went back to bed and fell asleep with almost the same rapidity as Oliver.

She was awakened just before dawn by a terrifying sound that turned her blood to ice. The unearthly high-pitched squeak came from all parts of the room, bombarding her senses like shock waves, and there was a sinister beating of wings close to her face. It was the most horrific nightmare she had ever had, and when she opened her eyes she was bathed in perspiration. But it was a living nightmare. The supernatural sound was real, striking her eardrums with the persistence of high-frequency torture, and as her eyes became accustomed to the dim light she saw the wings darting with rapid twists and turns in every direction. She had to find the lamp, but was paralysed with fear. It was like watching a horror movie, only ten times more spine chilling.

Slowly she eased herself up on her elbow, now fully awake, and within seconds of realising the intruder was a bat she was literally caught up in the most terrorising experience of her life. As she lifted her head from the pillow the bat swooped and she was convinced its radar-like powers were not coming into operation quickly enough to avoid her. It was going to tangle with her hair.

She screamed. Her body was rigid with fear, but somehow she managed to get to the window, tossing her head frantically, and her shrieks rang out. She was beside herself with fright, and the more she shook her head the more enmeshed she felt the creature becoming in the long strands of hair that were now caught painfully, pulling at her scalp. Thinking she could shake it off the thrashing of her head increased, but the tangle got worse and she was on the point of hysteria.

'Meredith!' Joss burst into the room, took one look at the nearly demented girl and covered the distance between them in a few strides. 'Whatever is the matter with you?'

He tried to drag her back from the window, but she screamed again in pain.

'There's a bat in my hair! *Do* something, Joss. For heaven's sake get it out!'

There was a sound behind him in the room and he turned, seeing the swift flight of a tiny creature seeking escape from the confined space it had mistaken for the hole under the eaves. He gave a wry smile and looked back at Meredith. A sympathetic hand gripped her shoulder.

'Stand still and stop being such an idiot,' he commanded. 'Your hair is tangled with the firethorn bush outside the window, and the poor little bat can't get out again while you're blocking its only exit.'

She was immediately still, but when she tried to stand up straight she was so caught up in the firethorn twigs it was impossible to move.

'I can't get away,' she said weakly, already ashamed of her stupidity.

He leaned over her to see what he could do, but the tangle was too great to unravel. 'You ought to have had enough sense to know that one thing bats *never* do is get in anyone's hair. It's just an old wives' tale. You'll have to stay where you are while I find some scissors.'

'You're not going to cut my hair!' she gasped.

'I'll have to, unless you want to become part of the fixtures.'

She heard him go over to the dressing-table and rummage through a couple of drawers until he found what he was looking for, then he came back to her.

'Please don't cut more than you have to,' she begged.

The blades clipped away at her hair, seeming to cut off an enormous quantity, and she was filled with misery. Except for occasionally having the ends tidied no scissors had ever been near it before.

'There!' said Joss at last. 'You can stand up now.' When she did so there were tears rolling down her face. 'It's all right, my girl, you're not bald. A bit of thinning out won't hurt that mop at all.'

'Oh, you're so cruel, Joss Hamblyn!'

'Am I?' He only grinned, recognising her reaction to fear. 'Come and sit at the dressing-table.'

He was speaking to her the way he did to the children and she obeyed him instinctively. She looked in the mirror, aghast at the mess her hair was in. The women in Hogarth's drawings were nowhere in it. A moment later there was a stir in the air as the bat winged away through the window, and she felt sick at the way she had made such a complete fool of herself.

She tried to draw a brush through her hair, but made no impression. 'I shall have to have it cut short!' she wailed.

Joss came up behind her and began massaging the tension spot at the nape of her neck until she drew in her breath and the hairbrush dropped to the floor.

'You have the most beautiful hair I've ever seen,' he murmured, lifting it away from her face and crushing it like silk in his palms. He picked up the brush and used it with deft strokes that soon restored the heavy mane to shining order. 'Don't ever cut an inch of it, or I'll want to know the reason why. It would be criminal.'

Ecstatic shivers cascaded down her spine and she wanted his manipulation of the hairbrush to go on and on. And was she hearing right? Was he really saying such wonderful things in that husky, seductive voice? She glanced up at his reflection. He wore a green silk robe which was tied at the waist but hung open at the top to reveal a wide expanse of bronzed chest where brown hair curled and matted. The brush hovered over the crown of her head and was still. She looked up further and met his eyes, drawn by a force stronger than anything she had encountered before, and suddenly nothing mattered except the fusion of their separate identities in a melting pot of overwhelming awareness. Her lips parted. Her breath was a whisper of incomprehension. She was lost somewhere in the depths of those inscrutable eyes, as if he was holding her prisoner and there was no way she could escape. When she could stand it no longer she twisted round and buried her face against his chest, her arms twining round his neck.

'Oh, Joss!'

He held her against him, his fingers caressing the back of her head, and she felt his mouth touch her hair. They stood like that for several seconds, her body pressed to his, and neither moved. The contact filled her with an emotion too deep to understand and she couldn't be sure whether the clamouring heartbeats blocking out all other sounds were hers or his. He didn't attempt to kiss her, made no move to stimulate any physical desire, and she gradually relaxed in his arms, lost in the rare phenomenon of experiencing oneness with another being. She didn't want to think beyond this moment. But Joss didn't permit it to last. Too soon his arms slackened and he set her gently aside.

'Get back to bed,' he said roughly.

Then, without further word or glance, he turned and left the room.

She stood where he had left her, transfixed by the extraordinary events that had left her too weak and vulnerable to put up any defence. Was it her uncontrollable fear of the bat that had deluded her into finding comfort in Joss Hamblyn's arms? She must be getting paronoid!

Like someone drugged, she went and closed the window before climbing back into bed as he had ordered, and she slept through sheer exhaustion.

In the morning it was the sound of children laughing that awakened her and on the blissful edge of incomplete sleep she thought the night had been one of vivid dreams that lingered into the first drowsy minutes of a new day. But the voices were insistent and she sprang up with alacrity when she realised where she was, guiltily aware that she ought to be downstairs

What made Marge burn the toast and miss her favorite soap opera?

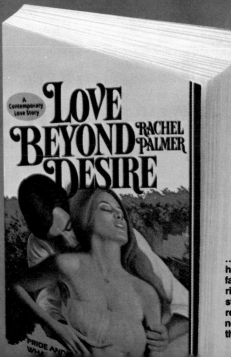

A Contemporary Love Story

LOVE BEYOND DESIRE

RACHEL PALMER

...At his touch, her body felt a familiar wild stirring, but she struggled to resist it. This is not love, she thought bitterly.

PRIDE AND
WHA

A SUPERROMANCE™
the great new romantic novel she never wanted to end.
And it can be yours
FREE!

She never wanted it to end. And neither will you. From the moment you begin... *Love Beyond Desire,* your **FREE** introduction to the newest series of bestseller romance novels, SUPERROMANCES.

You'll be enthralled by this powerful love story... from the moment Robin meets the dark, handsome Carlos and finds herself involved in the jealousies, bitterness and secret passions of the Lopez family. Where her own forbidden love threatens to shatter her life.

Your **FREE** *Love Beyond Desire* is only the beginning. A subscription to SUPERROMANCES lets you look forward to a long love affair. Month after month, you'll receive four love stories of heroic dimension. Novels that will involve you in spellbinding intrigue, forbidden love and fiery passions.

You'll begin this series of sensuous, exciting contemporary novels... written by some of the top romance novelists of the day... with four each month.

And this big value... each novel, almost 400 pages of compelling reading... is yours for only $2.50 a book. Hours of entertainment for so little. Far less than a first-run movie or Pay-TV. Newly published novels, with beautifully illustrated covers, filled with page after page of delicious escape into a world of romantic love... delivered right to your home.

A compelling love story of mystery and intrigue... conflicts and jealousies... and a forbidden love that threatens to shatter the lives of all involved with the aristocratic Lopez family.

Mail this card today for your FREE gifts.

TAKE THIS BOOK
AND TOTE BAG FREE!

Mail to: **SUPERROMANCE**
2504 W. Southern Avenue, Tempe, Arizona 85282

YES, please send me FREE and without any obligation, my
SUPERROMANCE novel, *Love Beyond Desire.* If you do not hear
from me after I have examined my FREE book, please send me
the 4 new SUPERROMANCE books every month as soon as they
come off the press. I understand that I will be billed only $2.50 per
book (total $10.00). There are no shipping and handling or any
other hidden charges. There is no minimum number of books that
I have to purchase. In fact, I may cancel this arrangement at any
time. *Love Beyond Desire* and the tote bag are mine to keep as
FREE gifts even if I do not buy any additional books.

134-CIS-KAF6

Name	(Please Print)

Address	Apt. No.

City

State	Zip

Signature   (If under 18, parent or guardian must sign.)

This offer is limited to one order per household and not valid to present
subscribers. We reserve the right to exercise discretion in granting membership.
If price changes are necessary you will be notified. Offer expires March 31, 1984.

PRINTED IN U.S.A.

SUPERROMANCE ™

EXTRA BONUS
MAIL YOUR ORDER
TODAY AND GET A
FREE TOTE BAG
FROM SUPERROMANCE.

↙ Mail this card today for your FREE gifts.

BUSINESS REPLY CARD

First Class   Permit No. 70   Tempe, AZ

Postage will be paid by addressee

SUPERROMANCE ™
2504 W. Southern Avenue,
Tempe, Arizona 85282

No Postage
Necessary
If Mailed
In The
United States

attending to breakfast for four hungry children. How long had they all been up? She looked at her watch and saw it was seven o'clock, got out of bed quickly, and wondered why her head felt sore. Then she remembered.

She couldn't bear to face Joss this morning. The way she had flung herself into his arms had been quite disgraceful, and quite unlike her. Whatever must he have thought? Her face flushed at the memory, and there was a sickly, churning feeling in her stomach. She hoped he would know that she would never, never have clung to him like that if she hadn't been so terrified.

How would he greet her? Would he think the unexpected sojourn to her bedroom in the middle of the night heralded a change in their relationship? Because it certainly didn't. Or was she deluding herself yet again? Something very special had passed between them in those dark hours which couldn't be shrugged off as unimportant. If he laughed at her this morning somehow it would be even worse.

But she needn't have worried. When she got downstairs, attired in a cotton housecoat of Ellen's which she had found hanging on the bedroom door, she discovered Joss so engrossed in domesticity he hardly spared her a glance. The baby was happily kicking in the carry-cot which he would soon have outgrown, Kirsty was spooning cereal into her mouth, and the boys were being instructed in the art of frying bacon and eggs, the smell of which made Meredith feel unexpectedly hungry. It looked as if they had all been up for ages.

'You should have called me,' she said, after good mornings had been exchanged.

'We let you sleep on for a while,' said Joss magnanimously. 'I was going to bring you a cup of tea presently.'

He was dressed for work, except for his jacket, and a vinyl apron with a gravy advertisement on it covered the front of him. He looked as fresh as if he'd spent an undisturbed night and she couldn't help admiring the efficient way he had organised everything, as if it was second nature to him. In some ways he would make a perfect husband. She sat down at the table feeling superfluous, and watched him handle the children like a veteran, fascinated by the way they rallied round him, especially the two boys. This was not the man she detested; the arrogant, high-powered solicitor who clashed with her at every opportunity and angered her almost every time he opened his mouth. This was someone she didn't recognise, someone she wished very much to know better.

'As soon as Mrs Burns arrives I'll drive you home so that you can get ready for work,' he was saying, transferring bacon from the pan to the plate for Shaun who had beaten Gary for the first helping. 'Gary, wait your turn and don't be so greedy.'

'But I'm hungry,' grumbled Gary.

'So is everybody else. It's time you started thinking of other people instead of yourself all the time. Practise it at school today.'

'Yes,' said Gary. Then his face creased into an impish grin as Joss gave him the second plate. 'Would you like this one?'

Joss laughed. 'Good boy! No, I'll cook some more for myself, but you can ask Meredith and if she doesn't want it I guess it'll be okay for you to dig in.'

'Thanks anyway,' said Meredith, 'but I don't eat a cooked breakfast. Can I do some toast?'

'Sure, help yourself.'

It was the happiest, homeliest breakfast Meredith had ever had, the kitchen soon ringing with family laughter, and when they were all sitting round the table it felt good to be part of this large temporary family. The sun shone in through an open window where a faint breeze billowed the curtains, and she found herself dreaming fondly of the future, a picture of herself in almost identical surroundings with only the faces of the children looking different. The fact that Joss was in the picture, too, was not of great significance. She was merely substituting him until the right man came along.

'I guess the baby must have been fed first,' she said, 'or he wouldn't be lying there so quietly.'

'Uncle Joss did it,' said Kirsty. 'Will Mummy come back today?'

'Not for quite a lot of days, I'm afraid,' said Joss. 'Will you mind very much?'

The little girl thought about it a moment. 'Not if you and Meredith are here,' she said, drinking up her milk.

There was a ring at the doorbell, and Meredith got up. 'Well, it's Mrs Burns this morning, poppet. That'll be her now. I'll go and let her in.'

She tied the belt tighter round the housecoat and went into the hall. Once Mrs Burns was in charge there would be no need for Meredith to stay, and she hoped Joss would be able to persuade her to move in permanently until Ellen returned. That would solve most of the problems. She opened the door wide, preparing an amusing explanation to cover her presence at Eden Farm first thing in the morning, but the words froze on her lips. The very beautiful girl standing on the step was a far cry from the motherly Mrs Burns.

It was Corinne Loring.

The two girls looked at each other a moment in blank amazement, then Corinne's finely plucked eyebrows lifted expressively.

'Well, well, well!' she said. 'I never thought I'd live to see the day our impeccable Miss Paxton would answer the door looking as if she'd just fallen out of bed. I hope Ellen is getting breakfast. I've just flown in from Tokyo and I'm hungry and exhausted.'

'Ellen is away,' said Meredith, finding her voice. 'But Joss is here.'

Realising it was someone other than Mrs Burns at the door, Joss came out into the hall. Corinne looked at him, bewilderment obvious even beneath the imperious frigidity. Then her glance returned to Meredith, incredibly hostile as the apparent situation dawned on her.

'You bitch!' she hissed, as she swept indoors.

CHAPTER SIX

'Joss *darling*!' Corinne exclaimed, lifting her face to be kissed. 'It's so wonderful to see you. Obviously you didn't expect me back so soon.'

Meredith hurried past them and shooed the children back to the kitchen table to finish their breakfasts. Joss would hardly want the reunion with his beloved Corinne played in front of an audience, and she certainly didn't want to watch it herself. She wished she could close her eyes, murmur a magic word and find herself transported to some other place, anywhere but here. Or better still, have Corinne removed before she had a chance to make her presence felt, because she couldn't have arrived at a more inopportune moment. Too late. She was already standing on the threshold of the kitchen, surveying the scene disdainfully.

'What a cosy little domestic picture,' she said, her high, ringing tone more affected than usual. 'Joss darling, whatever mess have you got yourself into? It's a good job I was able to leave Tokyo earlier than I expected.'

'An emergency cropped up yesterday,' Joss explained. Yesterday! Was it really only that short time ago? He told her about Ian and how Ellen had had to fly off immediately. 'Meredith rose to the occasion splendidly. I don't know what we should have done without her.'

'Well, *I'm* here now, so all your troubles are over. I shall just adore looking after Kirsty and that peach of a baby. I've brought them such a lot of presents.' She stopped, noting the two boys who gazed at her wide-eyed. 'Who are these?'

Joss spoke to them more sharply than usual. 'Gary, Shaun, where are your manners? Stand up politely and say hello to Mrs Loring.'

They didn't smile. After a murmured greeting they hurriedly sat down again and returned to their breakfast.

'But who are they? Where do they come from?' asked Corinne, distaste registered in every inflection.

Meredith went round the table and pressed the boys' shoulders reassuringly.

'These are Ellen's foster-children,' she said. 'They're super kids, and if it was possible to adopt them we probably would.'

'Hey, now wait a minute. . . .' Joss protested.

She couldn't have said anything more ridiculous, and the moment the words were out she wanted to recall them. The boys lifted their heads in surprise. Corinne stared in undisguised contempt.

'We?' she queried, picking up the most controversial word. 'My, my, things must have progressed further than I feared!'

Joss was quick to put things right. 'I imagine Meredith was referring to her own family. Her mother and Ellen have great plans for starting a holiday centre for deprived children, but they wouldn't like to part with these two.'

'A holiday centre? Where, for goodness' sake?'

'We'll probably convert our stables,' said Meredith, without thinking. 'Unless Joss thinks *this* house too big to live in alone.'

His eyes narrowed dangerously, warning her she was going too far, but she felt slightly hysterical, as if she wanted to say something really outrageous.

'I shall not be living here alone,' he said, the depth of the look he gave her quite disconcerting. It ought to have been directed at Corinne. 'Don't you think it's

time you got ready to leave, Meredith? I seem to recall
we have a busy schedule this morning.'

He wanted her out of the way. The curt tone told her
quite plainly that she was an embarrassment.

She went upstairs, brushed the dried mud off her
white pants and put them on. The sweat-shirt was not
much cleaner, but she had nothing else to wear until she
got home, and no one would see her if she slipped
through the wooded footpaths away from the road,
because on no account would she remind Joss that he
had promised her a lift. She sat down on the edge of the
bed to brush her hair and was instantly reminded of last
night when he had done it for her. Apart from a few
flyaway ends there was no visible evidence of the
trauma she had gone through, and she had to make
sure her emotions were equally well hidden. She had
come very close to making an utter fool of herself.

All at once she realised there were tears rolling down
her cheeks and she couldn't check them. She suddenly
felt inexplicably desolate. The only time she could
remember feeling any misery comparable to it was the
day Piers had been killed, and then she had sat on the
edge of a bed like this, refusing to believe it had
happened. There hadn't been any close friends to
comfort her. She had been more or less alone in that
numb state of shock, except for Mac. Mac had been a
pillar of strength, in spite of his own grief, and she
didn't know what she would have done without him. It
had been the thought of never seeing Piers again, never
to laugh or squabble with him, never to touch him or
know the intimacy of sharing her life with the man she
had loved so much, that she couldn't believe. But why
was she feeling almost the same way now?

She heard Mrs Burns arrive and she didn't want to be
involved in another discussion as to why she had had to
spend the night at Eden Farm, so she slipped silently

down the stairs again while the children were providing a noisy distraction. But before leaving unnoticed she paused by the lounge door long enough to see Corinne in Joss's arms, both too engrossed in the joy of reunion to concern themselves with anything else, and the sight of them did nothing to restore Meredith's spirits.

She was late getting to the office, and when she arrived it was no consolation to find Joss's first client, the formidable Mrs Galmain, installed on an upright chair in the main office where no one could miss her.

'I have been waiting ... half an hour ... for Mr Hamblyn,' she said, in her imperious, stilted manner, '... and I don't like it.'

'Mrs Galmain, I'm so sorry,' said Meredith. 'Won't you come through to his room?'

'Is he there?'

'I'm afraid not, but perhaps I can explain. . . .'

'If he's not there, what is the point?'

She reminded Meredith of the Duchess in *Alice in Wonderland* and she wondered how she was going to find the patience to deal with her, but she had to be placated somehow. At length she explained that Mr Hamblyn had been unfortunately called out by the police to a very urgent and involved case this morning, though she didn't say how early, and that only something of such importance would account for his absence. As she had made it sound so completely unavoidable, Mrs Galmain stopped drumming her fingers and consented to make another appointment, extracting a solemn promise that it would not happen again.

'Phew!' exclaimed Betty, coming in on the tale end of the harangue. 'You handled that old battle-ax beautifully. Congratulations!'

'Thanks,' said Meredith. 'I'm feeling a bit like her myself this morning, which didn't make it any easier.'

'I must say you look a bit devastated. Have the children given you a rough time?' Betty asked, with unflattering candour. So the half hour at home sorting out her most attractive dress and making sure her make-up covered all trace of strain had been a wasted effort. 'Shall I make you some coffee?

Betty followed her into Joss's room and bustled round opening the window and testing if the pot plants wanted water. Her grey hair, newly set and blue-rinsed, was immaculate, and if the grey shoes and shirtwaister dress rendered her somewhat colour-less at least she looked every inch a competent secretary.

'Can't stop for coffee,' said Meredith. 'I'm late as it is. It's going to be one of those days.'

She wished Betty would stop fussing and let her get on with her work. There was a letter from the solicitor acting on behalf of Sid Frank's late daughter-in-law. Joss would want to see that first. She put it ready to draw to his attention as soon as he came in and clipped the rest of the mail together. The 'In' tray was piled ominously high. Betty continued to chatter, anxious to find out whether Meredith knew any more details of the murder, but when she could glean nothing she finally left. But even when she had gone it was impossible to concentrate properly.

At ten o'clock Joss phoned in. The Frank affair had blown sky-high and he had to deal with a new development. Would she please cancel the rest of his morning appointments.

'But, Joss, there are two important ones. . . .'

'You'll have to fit them in for tomorrow.'

'You're heavily committed then, too,' she said. 'I've already dealt with an irate Mrs Galmain. What would you like me to say to the others?'

He was impatient to be going. 'Use some of that

damned initiative you're so fond of telling me about. I'm late already.'

'That doesn't surprise me. Corinne can be very demanding.'

Now what on earth had made her say that? There was a brief silence at the other end of the line and she knew his temper would be rising. She had noticed how touchy he was where Corinne was concerned.

'There were one or two misunderstandings to clear up,' he said icily.

'Which I hope you did to her satisfaction.' The frost in Meredith's tone matched his.

'Of course,' he said. 'And I'm sure you'll be relieved to know that she has no other engagements at present and is happy to stay on and look after the children until Ellen comes home. So now you can give the work in hand your full attention, and anything else can be discussed later. I shall be at Malvern Cottages for the next hour at least.'

He slammed down the phone before she could utter a rejoinder, but she muttered 'How nice for you' into the deaf receiver before putting it back on the rest.

There was a peculiar sinking feeling in her stomach. She tried to diagnose it and decided that anger at the way Joss had spoken to her had made it worse, so it must be due to temper. She had to calm down because it was obviously going to be one of those mornings. She didn't care twopence about his passion for Corinne Loring, she told herself sternly. If he wanted to court disaster it was his own lookout, and no doubt he was overjoyed that she was staying on, but he needn't have made his relief so plain when he told her, as if another night under the same roof as Meredith Paxton would have been quite intolerable. That was all the thanks you got for trying to help someone. Rude, ungrateful beast! She detested him.

Interruptions followed one on top of the other, but the next one of significance was announced by a commotion in the outer office which Meredith tried to ignore. She was in no mood to soothe any more disgruntled clients. But a moment later she heard her father's door open and a burst of excited laughter come from across the hall. Her own door was slightly ajar and when she peeped out she saw Corinne with Kirsty and the baby, greeting Howard as if he was a very close friend indeed, and Howard was lapping it up. Her shoulder-length blonde hair hung provocatively over one eye and she flicked it casually aside as he leaned forward to kiss her cheek. She wore a safari-type pants suit which accentuated her willowy figure, poor little Oliver having a job to perch on her narrow hip. She lifted him more comfortably into her arms and took his sticky fingers away from her collar with only the merest hint of irritation. The charming maternal picture she made would alone have melted the stoniest heart, but mixed with her particular brand of sex appeal which she could turn on as soon as a presentable male was sighted, its potency was lethal. Meredith had no wish to see her father swallow the bait, and after the first effusive greetings she went out purposely and joined them.

'Isn't this a lovely surprise?' her father smiled. 'We weren't expecting Corinne back for another fortnight.'

'Yes, isn't it?' said Meredith, hoping her tone sounded convincing.

'I've been telling Howard I shall be absolutely in my element looking after this adorable little family,' Corinne cooed. 'And Howard, I think it's divine of you to want to adopt those poor wee mites up at the house. Luckily I brought back enough presents for *all* of them.'

'I beg your pardon?' said Howard.

'Adopt, darling. Meredith was telling us if it was possible to adopt the two boys you would do so. I think it's positively magnanimous of you.'

'Er—yes.' With diplomacy born of experience Howard decided not to pursue the subject just then, much to Meredith's relief. She felt like strangling the other girl. 'You'll be here to help Julia and Meredith with the barbecue. They'll be pleased about that.'

'Oh, I just love barbecues!' gushed Corinne.

Meredith said: 'It's a fund-raising effort. There'll be plenty of hard work to do.'

'But of course, the holiday centre for deprived children. I think it's a simply heavenly idea to have your stables converted for the purpose. You really are a great asset to the village, Howard. You do so much for everyone.'

Howard gave his daughter a very strange look, something between humour and perplexity, but once more declined to comment.

'The stables need extensive renovations and I haven't decided yet what I shall do with them,' he said. 'Now, if you'll excuse me, I've some rather more important property to see.'

Corinne was smiling sweetly, a picture of innocence. If ever there was a born trouble-maker she was it. The ring in her tone told just how much she had enjoyed stirring things, for she must have known both Meredith's earlier statements had been made on the spur of the moment.

'Was there someone else you wanted to see, Corinne?' asked Meredith, when her father had gone.

'Yes, darling. You!' Corinne turned to Kirsty. 'I'd like you to wait with the girl in the other office while I have a talk with Meredith. We have a few things to put straight.'

Kirsty wailed, but was bundled into reception

regardless of whether anyone could spare the time to look after her, and before Meredith could protest she found herself being propelled back into Joss's room. Corinne shut the door firmly and dumped Oliver in the armchair.

'What I have to say to you, Meredith, isn't fit for young ears. In short, keep your hands off Joss. You may have had Piers eating out of them, but Joss is a different matter, and I won't stand by while you blatantly try to seduce him.'

Meredith laughed outright. The description was so funny she almost wished Joss was around to hear it.

'I don't have to explain my actions to you, Corinne,' she said. 'Joss has explained why I was at Eden Farm this morning.'

'In night clothes, and looking as if you hadn't had much sleep! You expect me to believe you had separate beds!'

'I really don't care what you believe. You're not married to him.'

'Not yet,' said Corinne, 'but I will be. So you can find yourself another weak charmer like Piers to get your hooks into and leave off bothering Joss.'

For a moment Meredith let the reference to marriage pass. She didn't want to give it substance, and she was too incensed by the insulting remark about Piers to worry about anything else. 'You're not fit to discuss Piers!' she flared. 'He had *your* measure, and he didn't have a good word to say for you.'

'And I sure had *his*, too. Piers loved Piers, full stop. He was a selfish, greedy little toad, and you must have been blind not to see it.'

'Stop it, Corinne! He's dead.'

'And you soon got over it, judging by the speed you've been working. I warn you, keep away from Joss. He's mine.'

The baby was crying, objecting to the raised voices, and Meredith scooped him out of the chair, rocking him gently against her shoulder. Her hand encountered a very wet patch at the seat of his baby-grow suit.

'As you've suddenly become so maternal, has it occurred to you to change this *adorable* baby's nappy since first thing this morning?' she asked, inevitably remembering how Joss had demanded the same thing of her not long ago. She was learning fast. 'Now if you don't mind, I'd like to catch up on my work. One thing Joss doesn't like is inefficiency.'

Corinne snatched the baby from her. 'Did you hear what I said, Meredith?'

'Oh, yes, I heard. But it's not worth entering into an argument with you. As far as I'm concerned you're more than welcome to Joss Hamblyn. He and I have a precarious relationship based on mutual dislike.'

'Well, it didn't look much like it this morning.' said Corinne, giving her hair another flick. 'Just remember I intend to marry Joss as soon as his sister gets back, so stay away from Eden Farm.'

'Oh, I will.' Meredith needed no persuading. 'I should hate to break up the love-nest. Perhaps you'd like me to take the children home with me so that you can have the house to yourselves. It might help my father to get used to the new ideas you've been putting into his head.'

It was a catty, sarcastic remark, quite unworthy of her, but she felt the need to show her claws. It did little to ease the anger boiling up in her, or the peculiar pain in her throat that made it seem as if she had to swallow over a brick.

'I don't need *any* help from you,' said Corinne, equally seething.

She marched from the room, chin raised aggressively as she went to fetch Kirsty. The little girl was waiting for her rebelliously and Meredith managed a wry smile.

So Corinne was going to look after the children until Ellen got back! She would give her two days at the outside before she threw in the towel; that was providing the children could stand her that long.

The confrontation with Corinne left Meredith more angry than she would have thought possible. So her father had been right, and marriage was definitely on the cards. She pressed her palms against her temples where anger was making them throb. She almost wished she *had* slept with Joss last night, though it would have been against her moral code. It would have served that supercilious Corinne Loring damn well right!

How Piers would have laughed to see Corinne behaving as if she was cut out for motherhood. Mac, too. It was quite incredible the show she could put on when she wanted to impress. Meredith couldn't bear to think of her married to Joss and living in that lovely house, ruining the warm, peaceful atmosphere just with her presence. She couldn't bear to think of her married to Joss at all, though if she didn't want him herself she had no right to be upset by his choice for a wife. It was none of her business, and she wished the wretched man luck. He'd need it!

For a few minutes she tried to concentrate on Piers, seeking to blame her unhappiness on to the cruelty of Corinne's spiteful words, but for the first time Piers seemed to have drifted beyond recall.

The phone rang while she was still trying to reassemble her thoughts, and she reached out for it automatically, not giving immediate attention to the voice at the other end. It was the police, and they wanted Joss very urgently. She told them he was out and asked if he could phone back, but that wouldn't do.

'Can you give me a number where we can contact him?' the policeman asked. 'He's needed at the New Inn straight away.'

The New Inn. Colin Frank. With customary discretion no other information was given, but it was enough for Meredith to know just how urgent the summons was, and her own problems were forgotten.

'He's at a house where there's no phone,' she said. 'But I'll drive round there now.'

'That's good of you, miss.' The policeman hesitated, then volunteered a little more. 'Tell him our elusive friend has turned up here, and he's armed. He'll know what that means.'

Meredith lost no time. Malvern Cottages, where Joss had said he would be, were down a stony track by the river, and she bumped down it in her car, her heartbeats becoming more irregular with every jolt. There had never been such a dramatic case in Edencombe before, and for the sake of the family she hoped it could be cleared up before it reached the ears of the press.

Joss was just leaving the cottage, and when he saw her his eyebrows shot up in surprise.

'I'm sorry, Joss,' she said. 'You're needed immediately at the New Inn.' She told him about the phone call from the police. 'It sounded a matter of life and death.'

'You could be more right than you realise,' said Joss. 'Thanks.'

He was in his car instantly, not stopping to explain, but he couldn't get it to start and he swore colourfully.

'You'd better let me drive you,' said Meredith, opening the door for him. 'The state this road's in anything could be wrong.'

Joss folded himself impatiently into the low seat beside her, still cursing. She drove back over the potholes, hoping nothing would approach from the opposite direction because he wouldn't take kindly to the manoeuvring that would be necessary in order to pass, and drew a sigh of relief when they reached the main road.

'I'd better put you in the picture,' he said, with some reluctance. The vital need for haste had communicated itself to her without explanation, but as his secretary she was entitled to know what had happened. 'Last night,' he went on, 'Colin Frank was taken into custody, as you know, and he made a statement denying that he was guilty of murder. He claimed extreme provocation and insisted the blame should be put entirely on his wife's lover. He was quite irrational and threatened to take his own life at the first opportunity because he said he couldn't live without her. This morning he had managed somehow to give them the slip, which was why I was not in the best of tempers when I phoned earlier. The old chap in that cottage seems to have been the only person Colin ever confided in, for some reason, and I needed to speak to him to see what light he could shed on Colin's character. It sounds like he's pretty mixed up, and if he's armed I'd say he's certainly a danger to himself if not to anyone else.'

Meredith drove through the village, impatient at the amount of traffic that caused delay. She felt like someone in a film, a sense of unreality lending extra confidence to her driving, but there was a strange knot of fear in her stomach that she couldn't account for. The Frank family were nothing to do with her, yet she had a premonition that she was about to become involved in this affair more deeply than she could have anticipated.

'What do you think he'll do?' she asked.

'I don't know,' said Joss. 'But if they're asking for *me* to go up there it sounds as if he's trying to make some sort of bargain. I don't like the sound of it.'

As they approached the New Inn it was plain to see that his fears were well founded. There were two police cars parked at the side of the road and a police van

stationed among the trees, from which a handful of
uniformed men emerged carrying radio equipment. One
signalled to Meredith to pass, his official manner
bristling when she pulled into the car park.

'I'm afraid I shall have to ask you to move on,' he
began.

Joss got out of the car. 'It's all right, officer. I'm Joss
Hamblyn, and this is my secretary. You wanted me up
here straight away. What can I do for you?'

'Ah, you're the Frank's solicitor.' He drew Joss to
one side and Meredith watched them talking, judging
the seriousness of the situation by their expressions.
Presently Joss came back.

'Colin Frank has barricaded himself in a bedroom at
the back with a shotgun and he's threatening to use it if
anyone goes near. The only person he says he'll speak
to is me, so I've got to see if I can talk some sense into
him. I think you'd better get back to the office.'

'No, Joss.' Meredith's reply was emphatic. Suddenly
there was a tearing pain through her chest and her lips
tightened with fear that bit too deep for mere concern.
He was prepared to face an armed man, with no
thought for his own safety, and she was terrified. 'You
can't go in there! Please, don't go!'

He raised an eloquent eyebrow, resenting her
timidity. He had a job to do, and no time to argue with
an anxious female.

'I'm following instructions,' he said, 'and if you're
waiting for me that's what you'll do, too. Obey the
police implicitly, you understand, and stay well clear.'

He went off in the direction of the back entrance to
the inn, and Meredith got out of the car, poised as if
she would follow him. A police sergeant came over
immediately, and she became aware that the area was
ringed with them, unobtrusively watching every move.

'You'd better come over to the van, miss,' the man

said, leading her firmly by the arm so that she was aware she had no choice.

The van had become a temporary communications centre and she could hear indistinct voices relaying messages and instructions from headquarters, current progress being related back with decisive brevity. To them it was part of a routine. To Meredith it was rapidly becoming a nightmare that made her encounter with the bat pale almost to insignificance.

Now she could see the window of the room where Colin Frank had locked himself in, the sun glinting on the glass. His father, Sid Frank, was talking to Joss in an alcove piled high with crates of empty bottles, and after a moment they both disappeared inside, accompanied by a police officer. The window of the upstairs room swung open.

'Only Mr Hamblyn,' Colin Frank yelled. 'None of you other sods are to come near!'

Meredith saw the man at the window and her heart nearly stopped. He had a shotgun clasped to his chest, his chin resting on the barrel, and even at a distance it was possible to see madness distorting his face. This was the man Joss was about to approach, unarmed, defenceless except for his strength. She pressed her hand to her mouth and dug her teeth into her index finger to stop herself calling out, bringing blood as her fear increased. It curled inside her, spread like icy fingers down her spine, gripped her scalp in shock waves as if an electric current was attacking every nerve. But the fear was not for herself. It was for Joss, and never in her life had she been so distraught with worry for someone's safety.

'Oh, Joss, Joss,' she murmured, his name repeating itself over and over in her brain as if it was a talisman. She closed her eyes and the words became a prayer. 'Oh, please, take care of him. Don't let anything happen to him!'

The minutes ticked by and Colin Frank stayed by the window, the gun still pressed to his chin. Every now and then it sounded as if he was answering someone who was trying to reason with him on the other side of the locked door, but he didn't move.

Huge black clouds hung over the moors. The sun disappeared and the stormy air was heavy with brooding tension, every living thing waiting, suspended in a motionless silence like an ominous prelude to disaster. Strands of hair that had escaped the knot on Meredith's head clung in damp tendrils to her neck and it seemed as if perspiration oozed from every pore of her skin. Her breathing was shallow, her heartbeats hammering with a force that made her dizzy. The abnormal atmosphere seeped deeper into her, attacking her nerves, and she didn't know how long she could stand it.

There was a movement inside and the police officer came out again with Joss. Sid Frank lingered near the door. The officer came over to the van and reported failure to gain entrance to the room, his statement confirmed by a volley of foul language from the upstairs window.

'I said only Mr Hamblyn could come up here!' Colin Frank bellowed. 'If any of you bastards come up with him I'll use this!' He lifted the shotgun and released the safety catch so that no one could be in any doubt he meant what he said.

Another police man accompanied Joss to the van. He didn't even notice Meredith was there. In the confined space his tall figure dominated everything, dwarfing even the uniformed men, and he had to bend his neck so that his head didn't touch the roof. He listened a moment to the planned strategy, then protested.

'Look, I'm going in there alone, the way he wants it,' he said, his deep voice ringing with authority. 'I'm well able to take care of myself, and if you'll just keep your men out of sight he won't harm me.'

'That's all very well, sir. . . .'

'*I* can get Colin Frank out of there, as long as you give me free rein,' said Joss emphatically.

He argued with them, his hand to his neck where it was cricked uncomfortably, and in a short time he won his case. Meredith watched him, marvelling at his abilty to sway police judgment, and beset by an insane urge to try and stop him being too smart for the sake of his own ego. His self-assurance permitted no contradiction, that lofty pride proclaiming that he was always right, and the familiar antagonism towards him made her blood begin to boil. But when he turned to give her an unexpected smile she became too confused to think straight any more.

'We'll cover you,' said the officer, as Joss stepped outside again, flexing his cramped shoulder muscles. A moment later he was standing alone in the dusty yard, midway between the inn and the security of the police van, head held high.

'Okay, Colin,' he called, 'you win. I'm coming up to talk to you. I've seen your old friend Jim this morning and he told me all about the rough time you've been through. I want to help you.'

Colin had rested the gun on the windowsill, pointing it towards the yard with suspicious uncertainty.

'No tricks!'

'No tricks, I promise you.'

Meredith clasped her arms round her body, tightening them until pain in her ribs made her ease the pressure. Her eyes were riveted on Joss as he stood there unflinching, the gun trained on him, and she couldn't draw breath until it was slowly withdrawn with a beckoning motion to indicate acquiescence.

She tried to tell herself she would have felt like this

no matter who it was out there facing such extreme danger, but an inner voice scorned the pretence and dared her to admit the truth. She felt this way because she was in love with Joss Hamblyn.

She watched him move away from the spot where he had made his stand, no glance in any direction to betray the men in hiding, and she identified with him in a way no one could unless they were in love. The set of his head and the straightness of his broad back were outward signs of the strength that was not only physical but part of his character, and a fresh pain stabbed at her ribs as awakening pride stirred violently in her. His sensitive hands that had caressed her and stroked her hair were now by his sides declaring his good intentions as he took slow, easy strides towards the door, and the most extraordinary reaction of all was a sudden desperate impulse to fly after him and share whatever experience awaited him in there.

If anything should happen to him she felt it would be the end of her existence. She couldn't begin to contemplate a life in which he had no part, and when she tried to think whether this was the same desolation she had gone through when Piers was killed she was stunned to realise there was no comparison. Her grief for Piers had been genuine enough and she had felt lost for a while, but it had been no deeper than the sorrow she would have felt at losing a very dear friend, she could tell that now. Beside this surging, passionate longing for Joss that had erupted within seconds of this threat to his life, she knew her feeling for Piers had been a very lukewarm emotion indeed. In fact, she had never really been in love with him at all.

As if sensing the depth of her revelation, Joss turned once he was out of sight of the man at the window, and across the distance his powerful green eyes sought her out. She felt them bore into her, compelling her to have faith and not be afraid, but when he swung round with an upward flick of his thumb before disappearing through the door, she stifled a gasping sob.

'It'll be all right, miss,' one of the policemen said sympathetically. 'We wouldn't let him go in if we weren't reasonably sure Colin Frank is only a threat to himself. He trusts Mr Hamblyn.'

The minutes ticked by and the gunman continued to sit by the window with the weapon pointed defiantly at his chin, but he was talking to someone, so Joss was in there. Then a shadow crossed the backcloth and he moved.

Seconds later a shot rang out.

CHAPTER SEVEN

THEY wouldn't let her leave the van. She screamed and tried to make a dash for the inn, but strong arms held her back, while uniformed men appeared from all directions and swarmed across the yard. There was no movement from the window.

'Joss!' she cried, struggling against her captor. 'I've got to go to him! Please let me!'

'All in good time. It's no place for you until we know what's happened.'

There was nothing she could do but wait, and time had never gone so slowly. Behind her another man was in radio contact with the scene and she strained her ears to hear what was being said, every nerve in her body quivering with fear, but the one way conversation was too disjointed to make sense. She crept closer, and presently the man took pity on her.

'That's a brave bloke you've got there,' he said.

'You mean he's all right?' she breathed. 'What was that shot? Was anyone hurt?'

'Hey now, have patience!' With infuriating calm he started taking down more notes on his pad as the distorted voice recommenced, but this time Meredith was near enough to catch odd words and an icy chill ran down her spine. There was mention of first aid and calling an ambulance, but Colin Frank was already on his way downstairs, it seemed, with an escort.

'Joss *is* hurt, isn't he?' she persisted.

The policeman put a friendly arm round her shoulder. 'It's nothing to worry about. Frank was about to pull the gun on himself, but Mr Hamblyn managed to get it away from him just in time and the shot winged his shoulder. It's only a surface wound, and he saved Frank's life, for what it's worth.'

Meredith closed her eyes with relief and sent up a silent prayer of thanks, but she couldn't stop trembling. The incident was over quickly, before any wind of it got down to the village and sent newsmongers up to cover the story, and it was all due to Joss's courage. He wouldn't want any publicity, she was absolutely sure, and she was choked with pride at his achievement. There was no one in the world like him.

She watched a very subdued Colin Frank being led away to a waiting police car, dejection in every line of him, and anger rose fiercely to the surface at all the trouble he had caused. Yet compassion stirred as he was driven away, for all this had been brought about by love and jealousy, and who knew what demons could be unleashed in similar circumstances, when emotions were heightened beyond endurance. Until this morning she hadn't known herself that love could have such an overwhelming effect. Her whole system felt shattered.

The sergeant came across the yard.

'You can go up there now if you want to, miss,' he said.

She went out into the gloomy light just as the first spots of rain began to fall and picked her way between the crates and boxes by the door, her heart racing. It was scarcely half an hour since she had seen Joss, yet in that brief time her feelings had undergone such a drastic change she didn't know how she was going to hide them.

She climbed the narrow stairs, her fingers trailing nervously over the oak panelling, and she remembered her father telling her how Royalists had sought refuge here during the Civil War until the Roundheads came and ran them through without a shred of mercy. Blood had been shed on these floors before, and Meredith had the eeriest feeling that ghosts of those sad victims had missed nothing of the newest chapter of violence to take place in this ancient building. She had never felt so cold, and her feet dragged unwillingly up the last few steps as if something was holding her back in spite of her anxiety to reach Joss.

Two of the staff stood on the landing, numbed by what had happened, and neither acknowledged Meredith. She went into the room, her eyes immediately seeking out Joss amidst the throng of police. He was near the window now where it was lighter, his shirt off so that Sid Frank could temporarily bind the wound in his arm and stem the bleeding. A pain zipped through her temples at the sight of it, and when she saw his grey jacket on the floor with the sleeve ripped she knew it was a miracle she wasn't witnessing something ten times worse.

Joss saw her and raised his eyebrows, a wry smile lifting the corners of his mouth. She went over to him, trying to match the philosophical ease with which he appeared to be coping with the situation, but it was the hardest bit of acting she had ever done.

'Sorry, Meredith, but it looks like you'll have to cancel this afternoon's appointments as well,' he said lightly. 'I'm being taken over to the hospital—it seems this scratch needs a few stitches.'

'I can drive you,' said Meredith.

'Afraid not, miss.' The policeman nearest to Joss was adamant. 'This is a police matter.'

Joss looked down at her, and as their eyes met for a crazy moment it felt as if they were alone in the room. She was deeply conscious of unspoken emotion, as if there was something he wanted her to understand, but there was nothing that could be said in that small, overcrowded room. He put a reassuring hand on her shoulder, and where it rested there was a burning sensation, as if the sun had been scorching it. She had a tremendous urge to lift her shoulder until his hand was trapped against her cheek, but that was sheer nonsense, the sort of affectionate trick played by lovers, and if he knew how ridiculously her feelings for him had changed she would probably be subjected to seering scorn.

'I'll follow you, then,' she said. 'You'll want someone to drive you home afterwards.'

She wanted him to need her. The sight of his bronzed chest made her remember how she had pressed herself against him last night, and she longed for physical contact again. She was amazed at herself, confused, irrationally preoccupied with a mere gesture of friendship, which was all the hand on her shoulder implied.

'I'd rather you got back to the office and told Howard what's been going on,' Joss was saying. 'I don't know how long I shall be waiting around at the hospital, but if you could give Corinne a ring she'll do the running around. I've asked Mrs Burns to live in until Ellen gets home, so there won't be any problem about the children.'

Meredith shrugged his hand away, the dictatorial tone cutting at her raw nerves like a knife, and she was brought back to reality with shattering abruptness. It wasn't that she had forgotten about Corinne, but the events of the morning had pushed her to the back of Meredith's mind, and Joss's cool reminder returned her to earth with a jolt. Thank heavens she hadn't made a complete fool of herself just now and thrown herself at him as she'd been of a mind to do.

'I'll go now,' she said, lifting her head and making sure all trace of emotion was hidden behind the mask of efficiency she had trained herself to wear at difficult

times. She smiled at the policeman nearby, gave a curt
nod to Sid Frank, and turned to go.

'Meredith!' Joss called. She looked back. 'Thanks. I'll
see you later.'

It seemed like days ago she had left the office, but
when she got there it was still only lunchtime. She
managed to catch her father before he went home and
put him in the picture. He gave an incredulous whistle
and bombarded her with questions, only some of which
she could answer, and her head felt as if it would burst.

'Always thought there was something odd about that
boy,' her father said. 'I can always tell. Not that I've
had that much to do with them, but in the year they've
been here Joss has been kept pretty busy. I think Colin's
mother went off with another man when he was quite
young and it must have played on his mind. I guess seeing
it happen all over again with his wife must have just tipped
the scales. It'll be quite a tough case for Joss to handle.
Nasty.' He picked up a file of notes and put them in his
briefcase. 'Come on, young lady, let's get some lunch.'

'I won't, if you don't mind, Daddy,' said Meredith.
'There's all this morning's work to catch up on, and
I've got to phone Corinne. And honestly, I couldn't eat
a thing.'

Her father paused with an affectionate smile. 'Poor
Corinne, it'll be quite a shock for her. Fancy coming
here to find herself landed with a brood of children to
look after, and now a wounded fiancé!'

'Well, she doesn't need to stay.'

'No—o,' he said sagely.

'Poor Corinne, my foot! She took over the children of
her own accord. I was perfectly capable of coping. In
fact we were getting on very well.'

'Ye—es.' Howard stroked his chin thoughtfully and
his eyes lingered on his precious only daughter. The
way she had reacted to a casual remark had surprised

him. He hadn't known her fly off the handle quite so forcefully for a long time; not since she first took up with Piers Loring, if he remembered rightly. 'Meredith, you wouldn't be falling in love with Joss Hamblyn yourself, by any chance?'

Meredith's mouth dropped open and she stared at her father in disbelief. Was it so pathetically obvious that even he could see she had temporarily taken leave of her senses? There was no doubt about it, she needed to sort herself out, and the first step was to deny it hotly.

'What a ridiculous suggestion!' she stormed. 'You know I've detested the man since the first moment I set eyes on him, so why come up with that idea? I am most definitely *not* in love with him!'

And may I be forgiven, she added silently.

Howard didn't look absolutely convinced, but he had more sense than to contradict. 'Good,' he said. 'Because I should hate to see you hurt a second time. I have the highest regard for Joss as a business partner, but there's been no shortage of competition in the marriage stakes, and it wouldn't surprise me at all if even Corinne failed to get him to the altar, in spite of her high hopes. Joss likes his freedom too much.' He snapped the briefcase shut and walked to the door. 'By the way, your mother phoned this morning. Your grandmother's making good progress and they've found a nursing home for her up there until we can find somewhere suitable nearer to us. She sent her love and told me to tell you she's planning on having the barbecue at the end of next week. I daren't tell her about Ellen being away.'

'I'm sure Corinne will be eager to help,' said Meredith. 'If she's still here.'

It was difficult to even mention Corinne's name without malice creeping into her tone. She would have to cure herself of it quickly. Almost as self-punishment she made the phone call to her that Joss had requested, and somehow managed to make her voice full of friendly concern.

She couldn't stay in the office over lunchtime. She couldn't clear her mind of the terror she had experienced when Joss stood alone in that dusty yard with a gun pointing at him, and her head ached violently. She sat in his chair, fingered the notepad where he had scribbled messages in bold, familiar writing, and touched the phone, wondering whether to ring the hospital to know if he was all right. Of course he was all right. They would think her mad, and Joss would just about blow a gasket! She had to get outside.

Almost of its own volition the car headed up the hill again towards the New Inn. It drew her like a magnet, yet as she slowed down to pass it there was nothing to see except a couple of customers' vehicles parked innocently outside during lunchtime opening; no sign of the drama that had taken place there only a short time ago. Meredith went on up to the moors and stopped at the spot where she had broken down on her first day home, memories crowding in with such clarity she had a job to disperse them. Like someone in a dream she opened the door and got out, breathing slowly and deeply as she had been taught in the yoga class she had attended the previous winter, and gradually she felt calmer.

The sky had cleared since morning, the heavy clouds rolling away to the east without releasing more than a few drops of threatened rain, and as this was a particularly good viewpoint there were already several holiday makers parked at the roadside with picnic baskets and folding chairs. Meredith locked her car and started walking.

The damp, peaty soil covered in dark moss was springy beneath her feet. She kept off the main track and picked her way through heather patches, climbing higher all the time, and as she climbed she pulled the long pins out of her hair until it fell about her shoulders. When she reached the crest of a ridge she sat down. It was a perfect day for seeing into the distance, though country folk said it was a sure sign of rain later. If she could have seen as distinctly into the future, would that, too, have been ill-fated?

Far away to the left she could catch a glimpse of the sea, though an untrained eye might have dismissed the thin silver thread as part of the skyline. The sun glinted every now and then on a glasshouse or window with the brilliance of a fallen star, and there was hardly a sound except for skylarks. An Emperor moth settled on the heather near her hand, but was frightened away by a lizard that shot out of the woody stems. For a moment it sat there, fixing her with cold eyes, then it darted away into a crevice between the stones, hiding its nimble brown body among the leaves where it couldn't be seen. Right now Meredith wished she, too, could find a convenient crevice in which to hide, but that would solve nothing.

She closed her eyes, shutting out the sun, but bright lights flickered behind her eylids and she buried her face in her hands. Always in the past she had been able to work things out logically and plan her life so that everything fitted into place. Even after Piers was killed she had waited a sensible length of time before deciding to come back to Edencombe, knowing that any impulsive move made immediately after losing someone was likely to be a mistake. But suddenly her brain was refusing to function with its usual sharpness. She hadn't lost Joss because he had never been hers to lose, but the shock of discovering how much she wanted him seemed to have robbed her of all sane judgment.

Perhaps it was delayed shock that made her give way at last to great sobs that racked her body. The stress that had been building up in her over the past days burst like a dam and there was no way she could check the flow of tears. There was no one to hear her, or witness what she considered to be self-pitying weakness, and she indulged in the merciful release for several minutes until she had no more tears to shed. Then she sat up, slightly disorientated but filled with a new resolve not to let any man get under her skin again. She would work with Joss a while longer because she didn't know where else to go, be as nice as possible to Corinne, and bury her feelings so deep no one would ever guess her heart was breaking. And above all Joss must never become aware of the havoc he had aroused. Never!

At the end of the week Julia Paxton came home. She had somehow managed to wheedle all the news out of her husband, including Ellen's sudden departure for the Middle East, and had packed her bags and headed for home with all haste, convinced everything was falling apart without her.

'The minute my back is turned it all happens,' she said, awakening the house with her vital personality and lifting the gloom that had settled. She handed Meredith packets of shortbread, oatcakes and butterscotch. 'The sweets are for the children. And what do you mean by leaving them up there with Corinne Loring, who hardly knows one end of a baby from the other?'

'Oh, Mummy!' Meredith protested.

'Poor Ellen would just about throw a fit if she knew Corinne was in charge of her offspring. A good job Joss is there. What on earth made the girl turn up here again all of a sudden? How is Ian, by the way? Any news?'

It was always the same when Julia had been away anywhere. For the first half hour at least she didn't stop talking and hardly gave anyone chance to answer.

'I managed to get through to the hospital in Mosquadec this morning,' said Howard. 'Ian is out of intensive care and amazing them all with his tenacity to stay alive. He'll make it.'

Julia sat down with a sigh. 'Thank God for that! Will Ellen have to stay with him until they can fly him home? I bet those little mites will be glad to see her back—Shaun and Gary too. The first thing I must do is go up there and see they're all right.' She paused, clasping her hands together before launching into her next thought. 'Oh, and Howard, I've had the most wonderful idea. It came to me while I was driving down the M6 and I've been working on it ever since. It's a wonder I'm here all in one piece, because I got quite carried away!'

Meredith and her father exchanged glances. Julia's ideas were famous and usually involved family and friends in work they wouldn't otherwise have contemplated. She was looking at them eagerly, her bright eyes the same lovely hazel as Meredith's full of enthusiasm for her latest scheme.

'Tell us the worst,' sighed Howard.

'The stables,' said Julia. 'You've always been saying what a waste it is they're never used now, so I thought it would be a marvellous idea to have them turned into the holiday centre. I mean, if we've got property available we're part way there, and it would make it a lot easier to raise money.'

Howard groaned and Meredith started to laugh.

'You can't be serious,' said her husband, putting a hand to his forehead.

'Why not, darling? And what's so funny about it? I'm *quite* serious.'

'You'll never talk Daddy into it, I can tell you now,' said Meredith.

'She's right. What's the matter with all you women? Corinne, Meredith, and now you, all wanting to fill the bottom of our garden with other people's children!'

Julia looked not the slightest bit crestfallen. If anything her enthusiasm increased.

'Meredith darling, did you actually have the same idea? Well that just goes to show it must be really worthwhile.'

Meredith's heart sank. She had already had words with her father and had a job to convince him it had all been a misunderstanding, and now here was her mother coming up with the plan for real. The last thing she wanted was to have the stables turned into anything else. It would be wrong.

'No, Mummy, I didn't think of it,' she said. 'It was a spur of the moment mistake I made that landed me in trouble, and I'm afraid I agree with Daddy—it would be quite impracticable.'

Julia pouted prettily. 'Oh, how mean of you both!'

'What you don't seem to realise, Julia, is that you can't just open up a home for anybody, no matter how worthy the cause. It would have to go before the Parish Council first, and then planning permission would have to be passed. There would be any amount of difficulties. . . .'

'Which could all be overcome,' insisted Julia, with incredible optimism. She launched into a list of details and described her plans so vividly Meredith found herself becoming interested in spite of everything. 'Just think of all the happiness we'd be giving those poor unfortunate children who don't know what it's like to run around in countryside like this. We're too selfish. We ought to be sharing some of the lovely things we take for granted.'

Meredith listened, and was gradually carried along on the tide of excitement her mother inspired until a similar excitement stirred in her, bringing her fully alive for the first time in days. Maybe this was just what she needed, a project that was so absorbing it would take her mind off Joss Hamblyn. She would devote all her energy to it and leave herself no time to think of anything else. Oh, yes, this was going to be the answer.

She went to Julia and surprised her with an enormous hug, for Meredith was not normally demonstrative.

'You're right, Mummy, we *are* selfish, and maybe it was an inspired mistake I made after all. I'll help you to talk Daddy round, and we'll go all out to get the barbecue organised for next weekend so that the fund can get under way.'

Her mother was almost in tears with pleasure. 'Darling, I knew you would! And I'll get on to Joss. He'll want to be involved, I'm sure.'

'Hey, now, wait!' Howard exclaimed. 'Women! First, Julia, let me tell you what happened to Joss. . . .'

Meredith left them and went up to her room. If she wanted proof that a distracting occupation was needed she had only to examine her feelings at the mere mention of Joss's name.

Joss had refused to rest after the stitches had been put in his arm. His work schedule was unaltered, and after the first day he had discarded the sling, which he found too embarrassing.

'It impedes my work, and interferes with my love life,' he had said, when Meredith had questioned the wisdom of doing without it, and had lifted his arm without too much trouble so that he could grasp her round the waist. She whipped free as if she had been scalded.

'I don't want to know anything about your love life,' she said, her skin feeling strangely raw where his fingers had pressed through the thin material of her skirt for that brief moment. 'I don't like sordid fiction.'

He had roared with laughter, and she had felt like hitting him. Even if she hadn't been in love with him she wouldn't have wanted to hear flippant references to his relationship with Corinne, who was now wearing a very beautiful diamond engagement ring.

Meredith opened her window wide and leaned on the sill, propping her chin in her hands. The rash promise she had made her mother was already becoming a doubt in her mind. Oh, she wanted to work for the holiday centre, no question of that, but the stables meant a lot to her and she must have been mad to agree with their conversion. There had to be an alternative site for the scheme somewhere.

The fruit on the cherry tree was ripening fast and if it wasn't picked in the next few days the birds would swoop. A blackbird tilted its head at her and winked a beady eye before nipping a cherry into its beak, leaving the stone hanging cheekily bare on its stem. Meredith loved the garden. She loved to watch sunlight on cobwebs spun between the hydrangea blooms and glisten on raindrops on the magnolia leaves. She liked to listen to the bees in the escallonia bushes by the wall and watch white and yellow butterflies in the buddleia. If all this had to be sacrificed to make room for a modern development she would have to go back to opposing it strongly, but if there was some other way of sharing the garden and stables with children like Shaun and Gary, she would work for it wholeheartedly. It was something she would have to think about and discuss with her mother before any definite plans were put forward. Meanwhile, the barbecue sounded as if it could be fun.

Next day Meredith tried not to brood over the project, and was glad of a complicated report which Joss had left her to wrestle with while he was away for the day. Life had never been so full of problems when she was in London, or if it had been they had belonged primarily to Piers and she had not been so deeply involved. It was much easier to sit on the sidelines and offer wise advice. Wisdom seemed to have deserted her now that she needed it herself, and she felt as if she was wading in a fast-flowing stream, being taken along on an ever-increasing current which threatened to sweep her off her feet because she hadn't the strength to fight it.

The weather was at its seasonal worst. A stiff breeze had been blowing all day, and by evening it had turned into a gale, bending the trees and spoiling the flowers, howling across the moor with relentless fury. Meredith didn't like the wind. It made her restless and on edge at any time, but in her present mood she found the incessant pounding of it driving her nearly mad.

Howard was at a meeting, and Julia had gone up to Eden Farm straight after dinner to make quite certain the children were being put to bed on time and didn't need anything, so there was no one in the house except Meredith. The gale bombarded the windows, and she could hear it above a particularly loud rendering of a Wagner overture which she had put on with mutinous satisfaction, thinking it would be suitable opposition. With an exasperated sigh she turned it off again and decided she had to get out of the house. Tying a scarf round her head, she set off down the path to the stables, battling against the wind. From past experience she knew that those stout old walls would provide a quieter shelter.

There was a deep rut in the ground where the heavy wooden door had dropped on its hinges and ground through the earth every time it was opened over the years, and this evening Meredith had difficulty heaving it. She managed to get it open halfway by pulling on the bar that slotted into an iron cradle to keep the door fastened from outside. It took all her energy, the wind seeming determined to thwart her every move, and she staggered thankfully inside, not noticing that the bar had struck at an angle. But she left the door open just in case it proved too hard to push from inside. The wind must have built up an extra layer of grit, causing it to jam.

And inside the stables she began to breathe more easily. Though she could still hear the wind she felt sheltered from its ferocity as she had not done in the house, and the churchlike quietness within the old walls had its usual calming influence.

She climbed the ladder up to the hay loft which she had been trying to convert into something habitable, but straw had blown over everything and it looked as if her time had been wasted. There was a lantern hanging from one of the rafters, but she didn't need to light it yet. The summer evening might have the feel of November, but it was still close enough to the longest day for there to be a good light through the narrow window for quite a while yet. She picked up the notes she had made several weeks ago about Piers and started reading through them, confident that if she could get engrossed once more in compiling the story of his brief but eventful life her own peace of mind would be restored.

She had been sitting there perhaps twenty minutes when she glanced up and saw a figure approaching with long strides down the wind-torn path. Her heart contracted sharply. It was Joss, pushing aside branches that caught in his dark hair, and even at a distance he was too handsome for any girl to ignore, shirt open, tie draped untied round his neck and windcheater jacket slung over one shoulder. Meredith drew an unsteady breath, wondering what had brought him in the vicinity of the stables.

She expected him to go on through the gate and take the path up to the moors, though what pleasure there would be walking up there on an evening like this she couldn't imagine. Instead, he stopped at the open doorway, and she heard him come in. There was silence for a moment and she could sense him looking round, his aristocratic nose sniffing the air for confirmation of her presence, for he would know that no one else was likely to be inside. She kept perfectly still, feeling like a trapped animal. If she didn't make a sound perhaps he would think the door had just blown open and there was no one there after all. She wanted him to go away again.

At the bottom of the ladder he called her.

'Meredith? Are you there?'

The force of the gale was as nothing now compared with the noise of her clamouring heart. It thudded like thunder in her ears, deafening her to all sound except Joss's voice, and she trembled in case his feet sought the rungs that would bring him up here. She could cope with being in close proximity in the office, but in the hay loft which had always been her sanctuary, the thought of him near her was too unnerving.

'Meredith!'

He was on his way up. The ladder creaked under his weight and swayed slightly. She was sitting cross-legged on the floor by the narrow window, the notebook open on her lap, and she waited for him to appear. Her scalp began to tingle and she snatched off the restricting headscarf, shaking back her hair. A bubbling excitement welled up in her, creating an urge to smile, but she drew in her breath, bit her bottom lip and managed to compose her face.

Joss came up slowly, his green eyes immediately seeking her out in the gloomy light, and when he stood over her, legs astride like a ship's master, she was unable to move. He completely dominated that confined space beneath the rafters.

'Why didn't you answer when I called?' he

demanded. 'What's the matter with you, sitting there like a discarded gnome from somebody's garden?'

She giggled, easing the tension within her. 'I was working, and rather hoped you'd go away.'

When she lowered her eyes they focused on his legs. He had changed into beige cords which fitted tight over his hips and emphasised the strength of his thighs. After a second he bent his knees and crouched in front of her, balancing on the balls of his feet.

'What are you doing up here anyway?' she asked.

'I could ask the same thing.' He turned the notebook in her lap so that he could read what she had been writing. 'As a matter of fact your mother is at my house eulogising about her plans to have this pile of stones converted into a holiday centre. I seem to feature largely in her schemes, so I thought I'd come along and have a proper look. And I did call at the house first to ask your permission, but there wasn't anyone around. I guessed this was where you'd be. You like this place, don't you?'

'Yes, I do.'

She had never been so aware of him. All she had to do was reach out and she could touch his thatch of soft brown hair, run her finger along the muscles of his forearm, bend her head and let her lips seek his. She held herself rigidly still.

'So why did you let her latch on to that ridiculous notion you came out with the morning Corinne arrived? It sounded to me like the first thing that came into your head.'

'It was,' said Meredith. 'And my mother's idea was entirely her own.' She told him about last night's conversation, and he sank down beside her, stretching out his long legs over the straw-covered boards. 'I wish you could talk her out of it, Joss.'

He lay back in the hay, staring at her thoughtfully.

'And if I did, would you keep coming up here indulging in maudlin reminiscences? Why don't you bury the past? Life's too short to keep dwelling on what happened yesterday.'

Meredith closed the notebook and put it aside, but the intensity of his gaze was so disturbing she had to take refuge in pretence.

'I'd rather come up here and think about Piers than do anything else,' she said.

'Were you lovers?' he asked.

The question staggered her. He had absolutely no right to ask such a personal thing, and brilliant colour flared into her cheeks. He was quite outrageous!

'That's no business of yours, and I've no intention of answering you,' she stormed. 'How would you like it if I wanted to know which room Corinne is using at Eden Farm?'

Joss smiled lazily, then leaned up on one elbow and reached out with his other arm, forcing her back into the hay beside him. She was too surprised to protest and found herself meeting those unwavering green eyes than were full of sardonic humour as he leaned over her.

'You're more prickly than a hedgehog, Meredith Paxton. You weren't like this the night *you* stayed at Eden Farm. I can still feel the way you clung to me.'

Her pulse-rate quickened alarmingly, and where his fingers touched her skin they sent fire through her bloodstream.

'I just happened to be more scared of that awful bat than I was of you,' she explained, attempting to keep her voice normal.

'And are you scared of me now?'

A gust of wind more forceful than anything previous bombarded the stone walls with sudden fury, and with a sound like cannon fire the door below slammed shut. Meredith struggled to sit up, but Joss restrained her,

tightening the muscles of his arm so that it was like an
iron bar pinioning her down just as securely as the bar
on the door now imprisoned them both.

'We're locked in, Joss!' she breathed, alarm widening
her eyes. 'Please let me get up.'

He made no attempt to move. His face was only a
few inches above hers and the lines either side of his
mouth deepened into a smile.

'If we're locked in there's no hurry, is there?' he said,
maddeningly. 'We've been alone before. Is this any
different?'

Yes, yes, yes! her heart screamed out. That night at
Eden Farm she hadn't known that she loved him, and
any fear she'd had then had been abstract, undefined.
Now she knew exactly what danger confronted her. She
was afraid of herself. Joss was playing around, taking
advantage of his last days of freedom before he married
Corinne, and she had to resist him at all costs.

'Will you please get away from me,' she insisted.
'We've got to find a way to open that door. No one
knows where we are.'

'All the better,' said Joss. He had been leaning up on
his injured arm and pain in it made him wince, but he
stayed where he was. 'Because I intend to put Piers
Loring right out of your mind.'

The weight of his body was against her and his
mouth came down on hers, but though there was no
way she could avoid the contact she kept her lips tightly
closed, refusing to give way to the tumultuous urge to
respond. Keeping her eyes shut, her limbs rigid, her
teeth clenched, she battled with herself, fighting against
capitulation with all her will-power, but Joss was too
experienced for her. He left her unresponsive mouth
and trailed his lips sensuously across to her ear and
down to her neck, exploring the hollow that dipped
down to her breast before returning to her lips, which

now parted on a gasping sigh. It wasn't fair! She could hold out against him no longer, and with a groan she clasped her hands round his neck, drawing herself up towards him with complete abandon. There were not going to be any more moments like this, so she might as well enjoy every ecstatic second.

Presently Joss lifted his head, his arms cradling her now.

'You know, don't you, that if I hadn't left your room when I did the other night I would have been there till morning,' he murmured. 'You're a fascinating girl, Meredith. You ought to take more care. You make yourself far too irresistible.'

Anger gave her strength to fight free of him. 'If you're insinuating I threw myself into your arms for any other reason than protection from that ghastly bat then you've a mighty high opinion of yourself!' She tried to sit up, brushing her skirt with trembling hands that had to do something, otherwise she would have slapped that smug grin off his face. 'Come to think of it, if such a situation arose again I'd rather deal with it myself than have you come to my room.'

'Oh, Meredith!' The exclamation was derisive. 'Am I really such an abominable creature?'

'Yes, you are,' she snapped. But her over-active senses denied the statement, and her need of him surged through her body with overwhelming insistence.

He knew it. His index finger traced the curve of her mouth until her lips parted and she fell back into the hay, limp with longing. The look in his eyes was triumphant.

'Tell me truthfully if you ever felt this way when Piers touched you,' he said. 'Tell me if you were ever as intoxicated with him as you are at this minute with me.'

He kissed her again, brutally, until she groaned and responded, making no protest when he removed her blouse. And, as daylight faded through the narrow window, he made love to her:

CHAPTER EIGHT

EARLY next morning Meredith was on her way to London. The case stowed in the trunk of her car was crammed with things she might need; things she had thrown in without any care, because her only thought was to get away from Edencombe as soon as possible. And as she drove fast along the motorway it was difficult even to keep her mind on the road.

It was not all Joss's fault, she readily admitted it. She was equally to blame because she had put up no resistance, but the knowledge did nothing to ease her conscience. All night she had been trying to accept it as inevitable, for somehow she had always known he would make love to her, yet now that it had happened she felt cheap and humiliated. She had wanted it, crazed for it in that moment of madness, knowing it would be the only opportunity, and now she hated herself. And she hated Joss even more.

It just went to show how shallow his affections were, for if he had really loved Corinne he would never have indulged in a casual affair that meant nothing to him. And if he had had any respect or regard for Meredith he would never have allowed such a thing to happen. He had used her, wanting only to prove his mastery, his dominance over women, and she had let herself become just one more name on his list of conquests. So much for the noble ideals of cherishing a great and unrequited love! There had been none of that on either side.

The gale had died down in the night and now the sun was shining. The tempest had passed, in more ways than one. Meredith put on her sunglasses to stop the glare, her head already aching. She had only stopped long enough to grab a coffee at breakfast and give a fabricated explanation to her parents for her hurried departure.

'But, Meredith,' her mother had protested, 'you can't just go rushing off like this! I don't understand. What's Joss going to do? Does he know?'

Joss's name had been like pressure on a raw nerve. 'He'll have to find someone else. Perhaps Corinne has unsuspected talents in that direction too.'

Julia was immediately filled with maternal indignation, sensing a need to protect her daughter from whatever hurt she had suffered.

'It's Corinne, isn't it?' she had said. 'She's done something to upset you. Oh, Meredith, it isn't worth storming off in a state about, I'm sure. That woman is trouble, I've always said so, and it's a pity she came here.'

'She came because she's going to marry Joss,' Meredith had answered, with more feeling than she knew, and there was no need for her to elaborate further. Her mother had looked at her with keen insight, the truth blindingly clear, and if she took on a share of her pain at the unspoken revelation she had too much wisdom to speak of it, for there was nothing she could do to alleviate the heartbreak of a love unreturned. But her own heart ached for this precious only daughter of hers who had lost her first love so tragically, and now cared too deeply for Joss Hamblyn. She looked at her pale face, wide eyes accentuated by the dark widow's peak where her hair was parted, and marvelled that Joss Hamblyn could prefer the superficial charms of a predatory divorcee when there was such a beauty as this he could have.

She had taken Meredith in her arms. 'Go if you must,

darling,' she had said. 'But if it were me, I'd stay and fight.'

In that moment Meredith felt closer to her mother than she had ever done, a bond between them that made words unnecessary. But there was no way she could justify her weakness last night and she deserved no sympathy, so after a moment she drew away, fighting back tears.

With her father it had been different. He had followed her into the garage after a lengthy but useless attempt to get her to change her mind about leaving.

'It's inconsiderate of you, Meredith!' he had bellowed. 'It's unprofessional, and I'm surprised at you. I hope you've phoned Joss and told him.'

'No, I haven't, but he'll understand.' And how! she thought. It served him right, and she wished she could have seen his face when he discovered his secretary's desk was unoccupied. 'I'm sorry, Daddy, but something urgent has come up and I *must* leave straight away. I'm going to see Mac Loring.'

At the time it had seemed like a stroke of genius to conjure up that name. If he thought that was where she was going he wouldn't want to know anything more, and she was right. But it didn't stop him exploding into colourful language that left her in no doubt she had said the wrong thing.

It was fortunate her parents had learned nothing of last night. Thinking about it as she drove along, Meredith congratulated herself on having remained outwardly calm when it seemed as if the tale was being shouted from the rooftops. If it hadn't been that Joss was able to force open the long-disused hayloft door and drop down to the ground with the help of a stanchion, they might have been trapped there still.

She wished she hadn't mentioned Mac Loring. It had been a thoughtless thing to do and quite without foundation, opening up old wounds for no reason whatsoever. But now that she was alone she considered Mac seriously. She had taken off this morning without any definite destination in mind, vaguely thinking she would book in at a hotel for a day or two until she had sorted herself out, but Mac might be just the person she could turn to for help. He had always been a good friend, and she knew he would be pleased to see her. She would call on him first.

If only she hadn't sold her flat in London, then she would have been able to ask Mac if there were any jobs going in the Loring Group and perhaps settle back into the kind of life she had known before Piers was killed. She might ask him anyway. She could always look round for a new place to live.

It was late afternoon when she pulled up outside the large Georgian house in Belgravia where MacDonald Loring lived. She was shown in by the housekeeper who had known Meredith when she had gone there with Piers.

'Miss Paxton!' she exclaimed. 'My, but it's good to see you!' Her matronly figure in old-fashioned black was reassuringly familiar and Meredith stepped inside with a feeling of relief, as if she had come back to her second home. 'Mr Loring's on his own in the first floor sitting-room. Go on up and surprise him.'

She went quickly up the stairs, her feet hardly touching the expensive carpet which was held in place with antique stair-rods of polished brass, for whatever the state of Mac's fluctuating finances he always managed to live elegantly. Her knock on the oak-panelled door was answered straight away and she turned the brass knob, going into the sitting-room with a glow of anticipation. It was a beautiful room, pale magnolia walls accentuating gilt-framed pictures and a perfect oval mirror over the marble fireplace, dark crimson curtains touching the delicately patterned carpet.

'Hello, Mac,' she said, smiling at the broad figure swivelling round in a chair beside a leather-topped desk.

Mac's face lit up. He must have been about the same age as her father, but good living had taken its toll and he was overweight, though not excessively so, and it was possible to see how like him Piers had been. If Piers had lived another thirty years this was how he would have looked, because he, too, would have indulged in the good things of life that money could provide. Meredith's heart gave an unexpected lurch. She hadn't realised it would be such a jolt coming back to this environment, and for a moment she wondered whether she had made yet another mistake. But then Mac held his arms out to her and she ran to him.

'Meredith, my dear, what a lovely surprise!' he smiled.

His big hands enveloped hers, patting them affectionately, and she clung to him as if he was a lifeline.

'You said I could come back if I found country life intolerable,' she said. 'You were right, Mac, this is my scene. I've decided it's time I was in circulation again, doing the things Piers would have wanted me to do. There's nothing for me in Edencombe.'

She prattled on, making her voice light and effusive, but Mac knew her too well to be taken in by it, and after a minute he stopped her.

'All right, Meredith, tell me what's wrong,' he said, his expression changing to concern as he led her over to an armchair and sat her down. 'I'll get Dorothy to bring us some tea—you look as if you could do with some. Or would you like something stronger?'

Meredith shook her head. 'Tea will be fine, thank you.'

There was an internal phone he used to contact his

housekeeper, then he stood on the hearthrug in front of
Meredith and studied her, his eyes questioning under
the bushy brows.

'Now,' said Mac, 'who is responsible for those pale
cheeks and circles under the eyes? I know they make
you intriguingly beautiful, but I'd hoped to see you
looking happier by now. So who's at the root of the
trouble? I'll soon sort him out.'

'Oh, Mac!' She gave a rather shaky laugh. 'I suppose
indirectly you could say that you are.'

It was meant to be a joke. If Mac and Corinne hadn't
been divorced, Joss would not have met Corinne again
and then perhaps he would have really cared about
Meredith. She gave Mac a mischievous grin, expecting
him to respond in his usual teasing fashion, but to her
surprise his face clouded and he stared at her with more
than a hint of suspicion. She didn't understand it.

'What have you been hearing?' he demanded.

'Hearing? I don't know what you mean.'

He fingered the heavy jowls that made his collar
appear too tight, rubbing them thoughtfully. 'You
always were a clever girl, Meredith. Piers was right to
trust your head for business.'

He went over to the desk abruptly and folded up
some papers he had been studying when she came in,
putting them into a side drawer which he then locked
and pocketed the key. She was puzzled, and not a little
worried. The words she had uttered so casually seemed
to have had some significance she knew nothing about
and had obviously worried him. Somehow she had to
put things right.

She got up from the chair. 'Mac, I'm sorry, I don't
know what you're on about.' She had no wish to know
the first thing about his precarious business ventures,
and if he was already gumming up the works of the
Piers Loring Group that was his lookout. 'You were

right, I've got problems, but they're to do with the heart, and I assure you I've no inclination to become involved in big business affairs again, if that's what's worrying you, though I might not say no to a job if you had one to offer me. I don't need the money, but I do need to keep occupied.'

He hesitated, his eyes still narrow as he contemplated whether she was being genuine. Then he bounced back to his normal boyish good humour.

'So you've got love troubles, have you?' he chuckled, slapping his hands on his girth and standing in front of her again like a cuddly teddy-bear. 'Well, I can understand you coming to your Uncle MacDonald, because nobody knows more about them than me. But I can't think why I'm even indirectly responsible for yours. Enlighten me.'

She didn't know how to begin. His odd behaviour had left her feeling tense and unsure of herself, and she was glad when the housekeeper knocked and came in with the tea tray.

'It was just a silly remark,' she said, pouring tea from the Royal Doulton pot as soon as Dorothy had left the room again. 'Of course it hasn't got anything to do with you.'

Mac plumped down on the low couch and regarded her owlishly. 'But you must think there's something I can do, or you wouldn't have come.'

Meredith felt awkward, not knowing how to answer. What *had* been in her mind when she scurried in search of Mac Loring? It surely hadn't been merely for old times' sake, so there must have been an obscure motive, like a wild, preposterous hope that he would listen to her story and be sympathetic to the point of offering to do something about Corinne. She hadn't realised she was capable of harbouring such devious ideas, and the very childishness of it appalled her. But Mac deserved an explanation.

'I don't know why I came, Mac,' she said, with a sigh. 'I needed a friend and you seemed the one to turn to, but it didn't occur to me that I'd be adding to an intrigue that's involved enough already. You see, like a fool I've fallen in love with Joss Hamblyn.'

'Joss Hamblyn?' he repeated vaguely. Then: 'Joss Hamblyn! That ... that bastard of a solicitor who defended Corinne and set me back a pretty penny!' His face reddened alarmingly and he thumped the cushion beside him as if he wished it was Joss's solar plexus. 'No wonder you're calling yourself a fool! That's just what I'd call you, too. But he must be an even bigger one if he doesn't want you. Why doesn't he?'

Oh, no! thought Meredith, suddenly aware of the enormity of what she was doing. What if he still cared about Corinne? It would hurt him to know that she intended to get married again.

'He ... he loves someone else,' she faltered. 'My mother said I ought to stay and fight if I want him, but I figured the odds against me are too great. And anyway, I don't know if I even *like* the wretched man any more. How stupid can you get!'

Mac flattened his back against the cushions, as if they were a wall he was up against, and looked shrewdly at his beautiful young visitor who was now kneeling on the hearthrug, imploring him silently to understand. And he did understand, vividly.

'Corinne,' he breathed.

Meredith nodded.

The gilt clock with rearing horses either side of it ticked loudly on the mantelpiece and she was aware of the sound of traffic in the street below, but they were only a background to the noise of her uneasy heartbeats, for the quality of his silence made her aware of the inner turmoil she had unleashed. He sat a

minute, staring through her as if she wasn't there, then
he leaned forward and rested his hands on his knees.

'There are two things I want in this world more than
anything else, Meredith,' he said, at last. 'The first is to
win my ex-wife back, and the second is to patch up the
quarrel that's gone on far too long between your
mother and me. Since losing Piers I've become
increasingly conscious of the frailty of life and I've
decided that his way was the only sensible one. If you
know what you want, go out and get it. And Julia, with
the common sense I remember so well, gave you good
advice. Why didn't you take it?'

'You mean I should have stayed and put up a fight?'

'Why not?'

She bit on her lower lip. 'I told you, I've decided he's
despicable. How can I possibly love him when I don't
even like him?'

'It happens, child,' said Mac. 'It happens all the time.
Do you think I don't know what a spoilt, selfish
creature Corinne can be, and yet I'll never stop loving
her. If you care for someone deeply enough you love
them in spite of their faults, sometimes even because of
them, and nothing will change it. Now let's have that
tea before it gets cold, and plan what we can do.'

Mac took her out to dinner, and by the end of the
evening Meredith was feeling in better spirits than she
had been for a long time. She had forgotten how nice it
was to be taken to a well-known restaurant, confident
in the knowledge that she was with a handsome
companion who encouraged her to choose the most
expensive items on the menu. She had thrown a golden
yellow georgette dress into her case because it never
creased and didn't take up much room, and when she
was wearing it the colour worked a kind of magic with
her hazel eyes, flecking them with gold. When she
changed into it in the guest room for Mac's benefit, she

knew he would be appreciative, and one look at his expression when he saw her left her in no doubt.

'Tonight, Meredith, I'm going to pretend I'm young enough to be the man you really want to be with,' he said. 'And we're not going to talk about either Corinne or Joss Hamblyn. We're going to enjoy ourselves. It isn't often I get the chance to escort such a charming young lady, and I don't intend to waste the opportunity.'

After the deliciously extravagant meal set off to perfection by a wine which Meredith recognised to be old enough to cost a fortune, Mac took her dancing. In spite of his weight he was as light as a feather on his feet and danced superbly. She remembered it was one of the things Piers had done extremely well, and when she floated round the floor with his father she experienced a moment of poignant sorrow. As if reading her thoughts, Mac slackened his hold and put a discreet distance between them.

'You know, child, I always hoped my son would marry you,' he said. 'I certainly wouldn't have done anything to prevent it, and I honestly don't think I would have held it against you, even now.'

It was a curious remark and Meredith almost tripped, upsetting the rhythm that had propelled them faultlessly round the dance floor.

'I wonder what you mean by that?' she asked.

Mac smiled. 'You'll know soon enough. And I hope you won't hold it against me either. More than that I'm not prepared to say.'

He insisted that she could stay in the guest room for as long as she liked and wouldn't hear of her going to a hotel. It was late when they got back and she was too tired to talk any more, refusing the nightcap Mac offered her when he went straight to the cocktail cabinet.

'It's been a very long day, Mac. And tomorrow I've got to plan what I'm going to do, so I need a clear head.' She went and kissed his cheek, as she would have done her father. 'Thank you for everything.'

'Goodnight, my dear,' he said, not attempting to touch her. 'It's been one of the loveliest evenings I've spent for a long while.'

'For me, too.'

He poured himself a whisky from the cut-glass decanter, and when he looked at her again there was sadness in his eyes, a glimpse of loneliness that was too deep for her to understand. He seemed to be trying to communicate something to her.

'Remember it, Meredith.' His voice was low and anxious. 'Remember it in the future when you may not feel so kindly disposed towards me.'

It was no good asking him to explain. The shadows in his life had always been mysterious, and even Piers had said his father attracted trouble like a bee to pollen. Whatever it was on his mind at the moment he certainly had no intention of disclosing it, so it was no good asking questions. But when she was in bed the questions tumbled through her head with annoying insistence, because in some way Mac's problems were connected with her and his anxiety seemed to hinge on her reaction when she finally became involved. She puzzled over it until her brain was in a whirl, but came no nearer to a solution, and gradually her own dilemma took over.

It had been cowardly to run away, and no matter what excuses she found for herself there was no denying that her flight from Edencombe had been the result of sheer panic. She couldn't possibly have faced Joss after what had happened, knowing that to him it was nothing more than a casual romp in the hay. By now he was probably laughing at her inexperience, and she could imagine his scorn on discovering she didn't even have the guts to brazen it out. Oh, it had all been just a bit of fun to Joss Hamblyn and he wouldn't have patience with her for thinking of it in any other terms.

She knew she was being positively Victorian, but Meredith's outlook on life had always been very straightforward, and she believed in the strict moral code her parents had taught her. It seemed as if once again she had failed them, yet she had to be truthful and admit that she wouldn't be feeling this way now if she and Joss had been going to marry.

She buried her face in the pillow and remembered her ecstatic response to Joss's lovemaking. Every part of her had been awakened by his expertise and he had taken her gently, knowing at last that she had not had a lover before. They had clung together in the timeless aftermath, too removed from reality to break the silence, until shock at what she had done made her claw at him in sudden frenzy.

'I hope you're satisfied!' she had cried, ashen-faced and trembling. 'Piers would never have taken advantage of me like that. He loved me too much, and he was content to wait until we were married. I hate you, Joss Hamblyn! I hate you, I hate you!'

She had ended up screaming at him, and he had slapped her face.

'I don't ever want to hear the name of that little tin god again,' he had retaliated. 'It's time you took him down off that pedestal and started using the senses you were born with. For Pete's sake stop making a martyr of yourself and relax!'

She had tossed her head defiantly. 'If you think you were doing me a favour it could be that you're right. You've made me see you in your true colours, and I think you're the most despicable man I've ever met!'

'Meredith, listen to me . . .'

'I won't listen to you!' She had been searching for her shoes and rammed them on her feet. 'What have you got to say that could possibly interest me? All I want now is to get out of here, and I wish I never had to set eyes on you again!'

She cried into her pillow. The bitter words had been used like weapons, wounding deeply, and she had been too overwrought to even try to curb her temper. Neither of them had uttered Corinne's name, but Meredith had been aware of it swinging like a dagger between them, the whole reason for the fight, because if Joss hadn't been going to marry Corinne the situation would have been totally different. As it was, she could only blame herself as much as Joss for the betrayal of another woman's trust.

In the darkness of the bedroom and separated from events by a great enough distance to bring about a return to rational thought, Meredith considered her situation. It was impossible to sleep when every time she closed her eyes she feasted yet again on memories of that forbidden love. They clouded her vision and made her certain of just one thing. No matter how vehemently she might deny it, the one vast truth was that she would never stop loving Joss Hamblyn. She was jealous of Corinne, and the thought of her at Eden Farm had grown to an almost unbearable pain which she could only learn to live with as long as the distance was maintained.

This was the real reason for her flight—she knew it now. The sight of Corinne with Joss, belonging to him, and belonging at Eden Farm, could not be borne, and as long as they were there together Meredith Paxton would have to live in exile.

At breakfast next morning she broached the subject of perhaps finding another flat, and ventured to ask whether there was any likelihood of a job for her with the Piers Loring Group. Her knowledge of the company was invaluable, as Mac readily admitted, but he was wary. Hasty decisions were often regretted, and he urged her to give herself more time.

'You were happy to go back to Edencombe and be with your parents, weren't you?' he said, and brushed aside her arguments as to why she couldn't continue to live there. 'I don't want to know any more about the other set-up that's bothering you. I have the very strongest feeling that a new turn of events will soon sort out that little affair very nicely, and to our mutual advantage.'

'I wish you wouldn't talk in riddles,' said Meredith, buttering a crisp roll.

Mac smiled at her with teasing calmness, his good humour completely restored with the morning light. He must have slept a lot better than she had done. He wore a silk robe tied tightly round his ample waist with an elaborate sash, and Meredith knew by Dorothy's surprise that he didn't usually get up so early.

'My advice to you, young lady, is bide your time,' he said. 'Have patience and everything will turn out right.'

'You sound very confident,'

'I am. It dawned on me last night that the very thing I've been worrying about might after all be our saving grace.'

'Oh, Mac!' She could have throttled him.

He poured himself another coffee. 'This morning, if you would like to, we'll go to Piers' old business suite and you can see for yourself whether you would care to be cooped up again after living in the country. I wager you won't like it. Then this afternoon I have a board meeting, so I'm afraid I shall have to leave you to your own devices.' He paused. 'By the way, have you phoned your mother to let her know you're safe?'

'Yes, I have,' she assured him, but carefully avoided

enlarging on the subject when his eyes pleaded for news that there had been no objection to her choice of refuge. Her heart ached for him, and she longed to find some way to end the ridiculous family feud.

She enjoyed her morning in the familiar surroundings, meeting old friends and exchanging news. She had stayed on working in the suite after Piers' death long enough to reconcile herself to seeing new occupants there, but she still suffered an initial pain when she entered the ultra-modern room where she and Piers had worked so closely together.

She was left in no doubt that Mac Loring didn't want her back with the company. He did everything he could to compare it unfavourably with her new lifestyle in Edencombe so that she would not think this was the greener side of the fence, and no mention was made to anyone of Meredith's expressed wish to return. She was treated strictly as a visitor, though made to feel an important one, and she came away flattered but in agreement with Mac's way of thinking. It would be wrong to go back there now. The pioneering days were over and it would be no more than routine office work, which would not offer enough challenge.

So what was she going to do? The afternoon loomed ahead of her, empty of everything except memories; but the thought of an equally empty future was too pessimistic by far and she knew she mustn't waste time indulging in self-pity. She was through with men. From now on she would concentrate on becoming a career woman, and the first step was to consider resuming her law studies. It would certainly please her father, and perhaps in time she might even become a professional match for Joss Hamblyn. Yes, that was what she was going to do, and having arrived at the momentous decision she felt relieved and infinitely more relaxed.

With renewed confidence in herself the next thing she

did was spend money on a new outfit. Her clothes had been smart but uninteresting of late and it was time she invested in something a bit more eye-catching to cheer herself up. Her first purchase was a full skirt of tiered white cotton with lace at the hem which she teamed with a gold and white sleeveless top, adding an alternative blouse with a lace collar for cooler days. The leather sandals she chose had flat heels and tied with thongs round her ankles, and a black paisley shawl of softest wool with a black silk fringe lent a touch of glamour.

She thought she had finished shopping when the cut-off Aztec pants and round-necked top caught her eye. The pattern was orange, red and brown, brilliant as a sweltering Mexican sun, and before she knew it the ensemble was packed and added to the parcels already in her arms. And it was the first thing she put on when she got back to the house. The pants suited her long brown legs, and she tied a rope belt of red silk round her waist, an orange scarf round her forehead with the ends trailing to her right shoulder. The whole effect was startlingly beautiful, and she wondered what Mac would say when he saw her.

But it was not Mac who was first to see the transformation.

It was late afternoon and Meredith was in the first floor lounge, her arms resting on the window ledge as she watched the build up of rush-hour traffic below. It was always a miracle to her how taxi drivers managed to nip through the tightest knot of cars and pause only at the lights. There were so many of them, and she paid no particular attention to the one with a single passenger until it slowed down and did a U-turn in the middle of the congested thoroughfare, which was risky to say the least of it. A moment later it drew up at the kerb outside Mac's house and the passenger got out.

The sun slanted on to a window opposite and
dazzled her momentarily as she moved her head to
look more clearly at the man who was now paying
the taxi driver. She craned her neck, convinced that
her eyes were deceiving her, yet there could be no
mistaking the tall, aristocratic figure that straightened
up and turned towards the door. A plummeting
sensation rocked her body and left her gasping for
breath, and she grasped the windowsill so hard her
knuckles turned white, for out there on the sun-
dappled pavement was Joss.

She stood up slowly, her knees weak as water beneath
the tight bands of the Aztec pants, and as she waited for
Dorothy to show him up to the lounge her mind was in
a confused whirl. What on earth had made him come
up to London with such alacrity, giving her no time to
get over the upheaval he had caused? She tried to
remember whether this was one of the days he had an
appointment in town, but it seemed like weeks since she
had been in the office in Edencombe and everything
about it was hazy.

The thought that he might have come because he had
discovered he loved her instead of Corinne took hold of
her like a lighted torch, setting every nerve on fire. Why
else would he come in search of her? She clasped her
trembling hands together, her breathing shallow and
erratic as she tried to compose herself and not let hope
shine too brightly in her eyes.

'There's a Mr Hamblyn here to see you, Miss
Paxton,' said Dorothy, standing aside to let him in. 'I
hope it's all right.'

'Yes,' said Meredith. 'Yes, it's all right.'

Joss came into the room, and it took only a second
for that wonderful hope to be dashed. His face was
hard, no glimmer of a smile softening the granite set of
his mouth, and his eyes raked her over from head to toe

as he took in the red and orange pants suit that had
pleased her so much when she put it on.

'You look like a tramp,' he grated, striding over to
her without any preliminary greeting. 'Which doesn't
surprise me in the least, because that is exactly what
you are.'

He tugged at the bandeau round her forehead and
pulled it free, jerking her head so hard that she screamed.

'Joss!' She pressed the palms of her hands against her
temples and stared at him, wide-eyed with fear. 'For
heaven's sake, what have I done?'

He stood before her, controlling the cold fury that
was worse than any display of temper she had ever seen.

'I came here with the intention of apologising to you,'
he said, his voice clipped with anger. 'I couldn't wait to
find you and put things right between us, and like a fool
I'd rehearsed all manner of things to say to you.' He
paused, drawing a long, furious breath. 'Thank God I
spared the time to get an evening paper on the station.
It certainly saved me from making the biggest damned
mistake of my life!'

'Please, Joss! I don't understand . . .'

She was close to tears, unable to think of any possible
reason for this savage attack.

'Don't you?' His derisive tone cut like a knife. 'Take
a look at that and you'll know why I can't find words
to describe the kind of girl I've discovered you are!'

He took the newspaper from his jacket pocket and
flung it down on the coffee table beside her, folded so
that she could see the headlines.

CHAPTER NINE

MEREDITH couldn't pick the paper up. Her limbs felt numb and she stared at the blur of words without seeing them.

'What's the matter with you?' Joss demanded. 'Are you afraid to look at the proof that you're just a cheap little gold-digger?'

'That's a terrible thing to say, and quite without foundation!' Indignation at last loosened her tongue. 'How dare you burst in here and speak to me like that! I don't even know what you're talking about.'

He snatched the newspaper up again and thrust it into her hands, forcing her to look at it. 'Read that, and deny if you can that it wasn't prior knowledge made you aim straight for Mac Loring and his money!'

Her gaze slowly left his face and travelled down to the words that had so incensed him. 'MILLIONAIRE DIED INTESTATE', was the preposterous heading. In the first instant it meant nothing to Meredith, her mind still preoccupied with the bitter accusations Joss had made, but as she read further he became no more than the bearer of incredible news. 'It has been revealed that the late Piers William Loring, founder of the wealthy Piers Loring Group which continued to expand rapidly under his direction until his untimely death early this year, died intestate. His father, Mr MacDonald Loring, now becomes head of the Group and inherits his entire estate, estimated at . . .'

Meredith's face became very pale as she reached the end of the paragraph and saw the sum of money involved, an amount so vast it seemed incomprehensible and became almost meaningless. She bit her fingers sharply, to amazed too take it all in.

Piers, with all the self-confidence of youth, had considered himself indestructible and had never contemplated death. What on earth had his financial advisers been thinking of not to make absolutely sure his affairs were in order? With her own legal background Meredith ought to have had the foresight to enquire herself whether he had made a will, but her outlook on life had been much the same as his and the disposal of Piers' fortune if anything should happen to him had never crossed her mind. And if it had she would have been reluctant to ask questions in case it seemed as if she was expecting a share of it herself.

'How terrible it must have been for you when you heard about it,' Joss was saying, his voice heavy with dangerous sarcasm. 'Just think, if Piers had died in that air crash twenty-four hours later *you* would have inherited all this instead of Mac Loring. You would have been an heiress, head of a business empire, rich beyond your wildest dreams. Doesn't it make you want to scream at the unfairness of it, especially as you were the one who helped to build it up?'

She stared at him in horror, the implications so far-reaching it was a job to take them in, but the first glimmer of comprehension chilled her with shock. If the wedding had gone ahead that morning before Piers took off on that fatal flight to Paris she would automatically have become his next of kin and everything he owned would have passed into her hands. But why was Joss so frighteningly angry, when it hadn't happened that way?

'Joss, I didn't know anything about this, I swear . . .'

His lip curled with scornful disbelief. 'You expect me to believe that? What a clever little actress you are!'

'I don't follow you,' she said. 'What difference would

it have made anyway? I haven't come into any money, so as far as I'm concerned nothing is changed.'

'And how that must have upset you,' sneered Joss. 'History has repeated itself, hasn't it? Your mother trusted her money with Mac Loring and lost out, and you've been cheated of any reward for the money and work you invested in his son's company. But *you* are not prepared to withdraw into an offended shell and do nothing about it, are you? Oh, no!'

His eyes glittered with contempt, and Meredith gasped as she began to see the way it looked to him.

'Joss, you don't *really* think I came here because I'd heard somehow about all this money? You can't!'

She was horrified. How could *anyone* think her capable of such tactics, let alone Joss? From the first moment she had known that he didn't have a good opinion of her, the memory of that day in the New Inn when she had overheard him talking still clear in her mind, but lately she had hoped there was a change in his attitude. The revelation that he was still as deeply prejudiced was as great a shock as the news he had brought, for it added to the humiliation of their lovemaking in the hay-loft. Love! His motive had been quite the opposite. There had been no gentleness; only a kind of vindictive pleasure in being able to punish her for being who she was. Yet why did he see no good in her? He had formed his opinions long before they met, without any fairness, and through no fault of her own his antogonism had taken on a new dimension. There was a violent stinging behind her eyelids as she blinked back the tears she refused to shed.

'What other conclusion is there?' he demanded. 'Your mother wouldn't tell me where you'd gone and I actually believed you'd just taken the day off because you were upset at what had happened between us.'

'So how did you find out where I was?'

'Your father told me,' said Joss. 'He was angry and ashamed of you because he thought you'd treated me badly, but I made allowances. I thought I understood.'

'You did. That's just the way it was, I promise you.' Her voice was soft, pleading with him to accept his first evaluation. 'I honestly knew nothing of this.'

She held out the newspaper to him, wanting nothing more to do with it, but instead of taking it he caught her wrist and trapped it in an iron grip.

'Then why did you come hotfoot to Mac Loring?' he shouted. 'Wasn't there anywhere else you could have gone?'

'Mac has always been good to me. He's a very good friend, and I won't have anything said against him!'

'Friend! You have the nerve to stand there in that outrageous get-up and tell me he's just a friend! Do you think I was born yesterday? I can see damn well the way it is!' His grip on her tightened and she felt as if an electric current was running up her arm. 'You lost Piers and his millions, so you've got to make do with his father. What difference does it make as long as the money is there. You disgust me!'

Meredith tried to wrench herself free, fury replacing her pathetic attempts to make him see it was all a misunderstanding. She had never been so angry in her life.

'That is a diabolical accusation and I demand an apology!' she shouted, her eyes flashing. 'And while we're slinging mud at each other just think yourself lucky I haven't accused *you* of rape!'

Joss laughed. It was an insulting, mirthless sound that exploded into the tense atmosphere like the report from a gun. 'That's funny! Coming from you that is the most ridiculous thing I've ever heard!'

She managed to drag her hand away, and the imprint of his thumb on her wrist was like a red branding mark which she rubbed furiously.

'I hate you, Joss Hamblyn,' she breathed. 'I hate you more than anyone on earth!'

'You're a liar,' he said. 'There's a strange chemistry between us that you can't deny any more than I can, and hatred doesn't account for it. I've only got to touch you and there's fire in your veins. Do you think I don't know!'

She turned her back on him and went over to the window, her heart beating faster than a tattoo of drums.

'Get out!' she ordered, seething with anger and frustration, because he was too perceptive. 'Get out and leave me alone. I never want to see you again!'

There was no movement behind her. The traffic continued to build up in the street below and the pavement was alive with people scurrying home from work, all concerned with their own problems. Did any of them feel as wretched as she felt now? Meredith wondered. If so she was very sorry for them. Her head was throbbing and she was shaking so much inwardly she had to cross her arms round her waist and grip her body.

Why didn't he go? All the ingredients of a violent storm pulsed between them, the deadly words they had already flung at each other were only sparks that threatened to ignite and cause a far worse scene. She couldn't look at him any more.

'Why did you have to come *here*, Meredith?' Joss asked, at last.

His tone had changed. There was a note in that rich, low voice she had never heard before, and it tore at her emotions. His tactics were altering, as if against his better judgment he wanted to believe she was in the right after all, but she was not going to be fooled into lowering her defences even a fraction.

'I had to get away from you,' she said.

His soft-soled shoes made no sound on the thick carpet and he came up behind her with the stealth of a panther, swinging her body towards him so suddenly she was unprepared.

'What were you afraid of?' he asked savagely. 'Wasn't I fit to touch you after your precious Piers? Or were you afraid of the passion I can rouse in you?'

She went rigid, rejecting the automatic response that surged through her at his touch; despising herself for the miserable weakness that threatened to overwhelm her.

She jerked back her head. 'Don't flatter yourself. The only passionate feeling you arouse in me is revulsion. Let go of me!'

She tried to fight against him, but her struggles were as useless as the fluttering of a trapped bird. One hand cupped the back of her head so that she couldn't escape the pressure of his mouth as it came down on hers with punishing hardness, and there was no mercy in him. She clenched her fists and thumped his back until there must have been bruises, but it made no impression other than to increase the strength of his hold on her, and gradually her fingers slackened. The more she tried to extricate herself the weaker her resistance became, and a craving to yield made her catch at his hair with feline wildness, but she was too aware of the danger to let her body relax even momentarily against his. He knew her weakness; would take advantage of it. Keeping her mind as detached as possible from the treacherous betrayal of her senses, she lifted her knee and drove it against him. He let go of her instantly.

'That's the kind of cowardly trick I would expect of you,' he said, after a second of icy silence. 'You haven't the courage to accept the truth that's staring you in the face. You need me, but you think you need money more. To hell with you!'

'I don't want anything you've got to offer, even if you were free to offer it,' she raged.

But Joss had wheeled round and was heading for the door without another word.

Completely stunned, Meredith wasted precious moments staring after his departing figure and heard him take the stairs at a run. Then she rushed after him, leaning over the carved oak banister to call his name because there was no chance of catching up with him.

'Joss! Joss!' If he heard her tormented cry he took no notice. 'Joss, I love you!'

The front door slammed and Meredith collapsed on the floor, her hand trailing forlornly over a carved cherub adorning the post at the top of the stairs, and she began to sob. He was a conceited, cruel, two-timing devil! Of course she needed him. He had become the mainspring of her life, the most vital thing that had ever happened to her, but no way would she ever share him with another woman. And she would never forgive him for the bombastic insults he had hurled at her.

She sobbed for some time, unable to check the flow of tears that Joss had unleashed, and crouched there on the landing carpet she knew she would never be hurt so badly again. It was the last time she would ever give her heart to a man. From now on she would concentrate on picking up the threads of her discarded studies and make a career for herself. She had finished with love for ever.

She went to the bathroom and changed. The Aztec pants suit which had inflamed Joss even more was rolled into a ball and pushed into a waste paper basket, and she stood under the shower until every memory of his touch was washed temporarily away. Then she dressed in a neat grey dress with a white Puritan collar that gave her a feeling of cleanliness and made her look a picture of youthful innocence. It was certainly not the kind of dress to inspire any unwanted overtures, and as she dried her hair and coiled it severely she knew she must never relax her guard for a minute, even with Mac Loring.

She understood now why Mac had been so mysterious, so anxious about the reason for her visit. The papers he had been looking at when she arrived must have been to do with the inheritance and he must have been very suspicious. Of all the untimely coincidences! Naturally he would think her full of resentment, knowing as he did how close his son had come to marrying her, and it was to his credit that he hadn't allowed his suspicions to diminish the warmth of his welcome, but she could see why he had done nothing to encourage her to return to the Piers Loring Group. Her presence there would have been acutely embarrassing once it was known that everything she had worked alongside Piers to achieve now belonged to his father.

She would have to leave the house before Mac got home. After Joss's accusations it wasn't right that she should stay under his roof, although she had no worries at all about her safety. It was the interpretation other people would put on her stay that had to be considered and she was not going to risk incurring any more slander.

She hurriedly packed her bag, wrote a note to thank Mac for his hospitality and assure him she was all right, then slipped out with only a brief word to Dorothy. Her car was in a garage at the back of the house and she drove out without any idea where she was going.

There were hotels, of course but she didn't want to stay in one if she could help it. Much better to find something slightly more permanent if she was going to stay on in London and look for a job. She drove around aimlessly for a while, her brain not functioning with its usual clarity. On street corners the placards now announced the destiny of the Loring Group in huge letters and newsvendors shouted it to the world. The value of shares in the company had dropped drastically. Poor Mac! No one ever seemed to have any faith in him. Meredith had left the paper Joss had brought on the coffee table, so she bought another, but only to read the advertisements for accommodation. She didn't want to read another word about the main story.

There were two that sounded fairly suitable, and she tried unsuccessfully to phone the first one from a phonebox. The second was an address in Knightsbridge, and it seemed more sensible to drive round there and see for herself. It turned out to be a furnished bed-sit of a superior standard which justified the high rent being asked, and Meredith took it, congratulating herself on being so lucky for once.

'When do you want to move in?' the austere grey-haired woman asked.

'Now, if that's all right with you,' said Meredith.

The woman scrutinised her, taking in the neat dress and hair, and must have decided she looked the sort who could be trusted. She only hesitated briefly, asked for a week's rent in advance, and gave her the key.

'Left home in a hurry, did you?' she asked, as Meredith wrote her out a cheque.

Meredith gave her a scathing smile. 'I was disowned by my parents, raped in a barn, and cheated of a million pounds by the man who once double-crossed my mother,' she said, with dry humour.

The crinkled lids lifted to reveal sharp eyes that stared in disbelief.

'Oh, well, just so long as you're not in any trouble,' said the woman.

And that, thought Meredith, was the way to dispel

doubts; just tell the truth. Not that Mac had really cheated her, no more than Joss had raped her, but the basic facts sounded too extraordinary to be anything other than a joke.

She rang her mother as soon as she had chance. Julia wanted to know what was going on, but she kept details to the minimum, not even telling her that she had seen Joss. She hardly thought *he* would mention it, so the less said the better. But the sound of her mother's voice played strange tricks with her emotions and she was suddenly very homesick; very much alone.

Yet not so much alone as Mac Loring. Meredith found sheets and blankets in a cupboard and began making up her bed, hoping the mattress had been recently aired, and as she looked round the room, which was cosily furnished for good old-fashioned comfort rather than elegance, she compared it with the house in Belgravia. Mac was already living luxuriously, but she had a mental picture of him in a few months' time, spending his fortune on pleasures that would buy him only fleeting happiness. He wouldn't be short of company for there would be no shortage of people helping him to spend it, but in the end he would still be lonely. She felt very sorry for him.

'I would have hated to have all that money,' she said to herself. 'It would have been so awful.'

She had enough troubles as it was, without acquiring any more, and by the time she went to bed she was too dazed by the rapidity of events to stay awake and worry any more.

She spent the next few days trying to acclimatise herself to the new situation, going through spells of complete dejection which could only be banished by seeking the company of old friends, and gradually she began to think of Joss less often during daylight hours. It was at night the pain was so bad. Then she would remember the pressure of his mouth on hers, the heat of him against her, and she would grow warm with longing for him, in spite of all her cool resolutions to forget. The feelings she had for him were scorching and destructive, yet at the same time charged with a yearning so deep she could see no way out of the resulting confusion. Living alone was perhaps not the best remedy, but she would have to get used to it.

It was at the end of the following week that Meredith had a very unexpected visitor. She had been out all the morning at an interview for a job with a big financial company, and though she had a good chance of getting it she was by no means sure she would be able to settle there. She was trying to come to a decision when there was a knock at the door. Thinking it was the young man from the room opposite who was beginning to make a habit of popping across to borrow things, she drew her lips into a prim line which changed to the rounded shape of surprise when she saw who it was.

For a second she didn't recognise her. The short hair had grown longer and she was very suntanned, but there was no mistaking the eyes which were enough like her brother's to make Meredith gasp.

'Ellen!' The two girls faced each other a moment, then clasped hands excitedly. 'Oh, Ellen, how wonderful to see you! When did you get back? How's Ian? And the children . . .'

'You sound exactly like your mother!' Ellen laughed, coming into the room. 'She told me where you were and I thought it was time someone came and looked you up.' She gazed around. 'This is nice. I like it.'

Meredith boiled the kettle and made tea, talking all the time. Ian, it seemed, would be fit to travel in another two weeks, but Ellen had been so lost without the children the hospital had agreed that it was all right for her to return earlier.

'If you could have seen Kirsty's little face when I arrived,' she said. 'I don't think Oliver knew what was happening, but I'm sure he was just as excited in his way. It was just wonderful to get home—I can't begin to tell you how wonderful.'

'I'm sure it was,' Meredith agreed, and was beset by a strange envy such as she had never experienced before. She didn't begrudge Ellen a thing, but the thought of being so rapturously welcomed home brought a lump to her throat.

Over a hastily prepared lunch they talked without ceasing, mostly of the miraculous recovery Ian had made, and Ellen's praise for the hospital couldn't have been greater.

'No one believed he would pull through,' she said. 'And he wouldn't have done if it hadn't been for those wonderful doctors and nurses. I was telling your mother . . .'

They talked of Howard and Julia, of Shaun and Gary, of almost everyone in Edencombe, it seemed, except one.

'Meredith,' Ellen said at last, 'you haven't said a word about my brother. What's happened between you? And why *are* you here?'

The sound of his name made Meredith catch her breath, yet she had known questions were bound to come. It was a temptation to open her heart to Ellen, who was one of the most sympathetic people she had ever met, but it was not her way to unburden her troubles on others, and anyway Ellen wouldn't want to hear any criticism of her brother. However, there had to be some sort of explanation.

'There were . . . problems,' said Meredith warily.

Ellen eyed her curiously for a second. 'It's Corinne Loring, isn't it?'

'Partly.' Meredith gave a brittle laugh. 'Honestly,

Ellen, when I saw you at the door I thought you'd come to tell me off because I hadn't kept my bargain about looking after the children, but I really had no choice. I was getting on fine, and then Corinne marched in and took over.'

'In more ways than one, I've no doubt.' The disapproval in Ellen's tone was heartening. 'That woman is an absolute menace! I could never understand why Joss never saw through her in the first place, but then I can't look at her with a masculine eye. It didn't take long for her to show her true colours, though, thank goodness.'

Ellen got up and wandered across the room, while Meredith quivered and waited to know what she was leading up to. There was an Afghan rug on the couch which she fingered with interest, lifting it so that the brightly coloured wools caught the light.

'Meredith, I've come to take you back with me to Edencombe,' she said.

'No,' said Meredith quickly. She hesitated, nervous of asking the immediate question that sprang to her lips, but knowing it must be asked. Then: 'What has Corinne done?'

'The best thing she could have done from our point of view. She's gone back to Mac Loring.'

Meredith's mouth dropped open in incredulous surprise. 'Oh, Ellen! She can't have done!'

'She has, my dear.' Ellen gave a gurgle of laughter. 'The moment she heard about the fortune Mac had acquired her eyes began spinning like fruit machines, and she was heading for the goldmine faster than anything you've ever seen. So now there's nothing to stop you coming home, is there?'

What was it Mac had said about his worries becoming their saving grace after all? At the time it hadn't made sense, but now Meredith could see very clearly. He had known that the lure of a fortune would be too strong for Corinne to resist and with it he would be able to win her back, leaving Joss free. He had thought it would make Meredith happy, too, but that was before Joss had appeared with his accusations. And whatever must *he* be feeling like now that the girl he was going to marry had gone running back to her ex-husband? If she hadn't still been smarting from the mental wounds he had inflicted she would have been feeling sorry for him.

'I can't come, Ellen,' she said. 'Please don't ask me why.'

Ellen's eyes clouded with disappointment. Her greatest joy was solving other people's problems, and her gentle nature would not accept defeat.

'Your parents are missing you dreadfully,' she said, her tone persuasive. It was equally persuasive as she added: 'And so is Joss.'

Much as she liked the other girl, at that moment Meredith could cheerfully have shouted at her. Dear, trusting Ellen, who saw everything through rose-coloured glasses, knew very little about her beloved brother.

'I'm sure Joss must be much too upset about the defection of his fiancée to spare me a single thought,' she said sharply. 'And if he told you what he really thinks about me it might scorch your ears.'

Ellen was puzzled. 'Fiancée?' she queried. 'What fiancée?'

'Why, Corinne, of course. They were going to get married as soon as you got back home.'

'Oh, Meredith, really!' Ellen exclaimed. 'Wherever did you get hold of that tale? I'm sure Joss never told you anything so preposterous. If he thought he would have to spend a lifetime with Corinne he'd just about die the death! A few weeks was too much. He was just about at the end of his tether when I got back. You ought never to have gone away.'

'They were engaged,' said Meredith emphatically. 'Corinne told me herself, and I saw the ring.'

'What, that vulgar diamond? That's the one Mac gave her. You mean to say she's been wearing that thing again?'

The two girls had been facing each other, each convinced of their own facts, but all at once Meredith began to see the cunning Corinne had used to keep Joss for herself, and she wilted visibly, sinking down on to the couch. If only she hadn't been so gullible! If only she had had the sense to verify the announcement with Joss, but somehow she had always managed to steer clear of mentioning it because the subject was too painful. And now it was too late.

'Corinne was very convincing,' she said in her own defence, her voice low and tight with emotion.

Ellen sat down beside her and put an arm round her shoulder. 'There, you see! Now there's no excuse for you not to come back with me.'

For a moment Meredith accepted the older girl's comfort, but she couldn't allow herself to be swayed by Ellen's insistence. There was no future for her at Edencombe.

'I'm sorry, Ellen, the answer is still no.'

Ellen gave an exasperated sigh and looked at her the way she looked at Kirsty when she was being childishly stubborn.

'Well someone's got to straighten Joss out,' she said, with unusual impatience. 'He's been unbearable since I came home and I'd got it into my head that *you* were the one who could alter everything. I suppose I shall have to try and see what I can do about it myself.'

When Ellen had gone the room seemed dark and dreary, and Meredith switched on the light. She went to the mirror and stared at herself without seeing any of the outward beauty that had attracted Joss. She was a fool; a blind, idiotic fool, to have let love slip through her hands, but there was no reprieve. Joss had stated his opinion of her with cruel injustice and nothing had happened that would change that. Pride would keep her as far away from him as possible. It was over.

CHAPTER TEN

.

LATE the following Saturday she was driving back to
Edencombe, her resolve in no way weakened, but lack
of clothes making the journey a necessity. She had
already refused a date because she had nothing to
wear, and it was ridiculous to go to the expense of
replenishing her wardrobe with new things when there
was so much in her bedroom at home, so there was
nothing for it but to risk making the trip.

She had decided Saturday was the most sensible time,
arriving late in the evening when there was no fear of
running into Joss. She would be able to spend Sunday
quietly with her parents and start back early on
Monday morning. That way she was most likely to
avoid any unexpected encounter with him. And she
hadn't warned anyone she was coming, just in case her
mother or Ellen got the idea that she had reconsidered.

She had done a lot of thinking since Ellen had come
to see her, and it hadn't eased her heartache at all. The
fact that Corinne was no longer at Eden Farm hardly
changed the situation, though it might have done once.
She couldn't say Joss had been deliberately misleading,
but he had never been open about his relationship with
her, and Meredith didn't trust him. If that had been the
only problem she would have come back before now,
but he had turned the tables and made those
unforgivable accusations. Never again would she let
herself be hurt the way she had been that day at Mac's
house.

All she hoped was that Mac was now happy.

It was dusk when she approached Edencombe.

Mindful of what had happened the last time she came home, she took the low road into the village, driving past the office with mixed feelings, but glad that she avoided the hill by Eden Farm. It was a warm, clear evening and she looked forward to a quiet dinner with her parents and time to sit alone with them and talk, but as she turned the corner towards Combe Lodge she was surprised to see a conglomeration of cars parked everywhere in the vicinity. And when she wound down the window and put her nose outside it wrinkled up at the unexpected smell of woodsmoke and charcoal.

'Oh, lord,' she murmured, her heart sinking like a stone, 'the barbecue! I'd forgotten all about it.'

By the look of things it was being very well patronised, and gusts of laughter drifted over from the garden direction. Meredith let the engine tick over a minute before going through the gate. It was a long time since she had been to any kind of party and the lure of it suddenly took hold, making her realise how very lonely and unhappy she had been in London. She would go in there this evening and enjoy herself, and if Joss Hamblyn happened to be around she would treat him as casually as everyone else; let him see she considered his verbal attack too contemptible to cause her a moment's concern. He was not going to keep her away from Edencombe. She had to conquer her antipathy and try to forget how badly she had been hurt, and the time to start was now.

The first thing she did was drive over a flower bed to get to the front door, and there was an immediate outcry from Ted, the garage man, whose job it was to organise parking, but when he saw who it was his face lit up. He came and opened the car door for her eagerly.

'Am I glad to see this little beauty back again!' he smiled, patting the roof.

'Thank you, Ted,' Meredith laughed. 'I presume you mean me. Or were you referring to the car?'

Ted chuckled. 'Both of course.'

There was no one around in the house and she ran upstairs quickly to her room to change into jeans and a blouse. Five minutes later, her hair brushed into a ponytail and comfortable sandals on her feet, she felt a completely different person. She was about to dash out again, no time to spare for romantic joy at being back in her own surroundings, when the cherry tree tapped at the window pane. She spun round on her toes like a dancer, and went to have a quick look at the garden before going down there.

There were coloured lights strung between the trees, giving a fairytale effect which transformed the garden and touched it with magic, but there was nothing mystical about the appetising smell of barbecued chops and sausages, and Meredith discovered she was very hungry. She could see people wandering across the lawn with huge hamburger rolls, and her mouth watered. She recognised one or two faces as they passed under the lights, but there was no sign of the exceptionally tall figure her eyes sought. If he had been there she would have been able to spot him straight away. Reassured, she left her bedroom and sped down the stairs, anxious to join in the festivities and start living again.

'Meredith!' Her mother's joyful cry rang out as she saw her. 'Darling, I *knew* you wouldn't forget about the barbecue. I've been telling everyone you'd be along soon. Your father's over there with an apron on, burning the sausages. Perhaps you could go and lend him a hand, then we can talk later.'

Meredith laughed, in spite of the sharp stab of guilt brought on by her mother's confidence in her.

'First, if I pay my money, can I have something to eat? I'm starving!'

'Darling, of course!' Julia lifted her hands dramatically. 'What am I thinking about? You've had a long drive. Tell you what, I'll spare a few minutes to come over with you, because I *must* tell you the most exciting piece of news!' She left the soft drinks stall she was running with Ted's wife, and linked arms with her daughter. 'Meredith, yesterday the most astounding thing happened. We heard that someone has bought an old property near Eden Farm anonymously and is willing to put up the money for our deprived children's holiday centre, providing we get permission. Fancy the scheme catching someone's imagination enough to finance it! It's too good to be true!'

Meredith agreed that it was, her mind working overtime to absorb the information and assess it, but she delayed making definite comment.

'So really this barbecue is by way of a celebration rather than a fund-raising effort,' she said lightly. 'And I can have a hamburger free.'

'You cannot,' said Julia. 'We shall still need every penny we can get. Your father and I spent last night talking things over, and we've decided the stables can be repaired and stocked with ponies for the children to ride when the centre is operational. We shall need your help, so don't go making plans to stay on in London. You're needed here, Meredith.'

There was a different ring to her tone as she said the last sentence and Meredith turned quickly to the hamburgers, taking a large bite into one as soon as she had coated it with tomato sauce.

'I'd like to come back. . . .' she began.

'That's settled, then,' said Julia. 'There was no need to go running off again anyway. I could have told you Joss wasn't serious about Corinne, and now she's gone you can patch up your silly quarrel.'

If only it were that simple! Julia had a knack of

reducing things to the minimum and expecting them to work out the way she planned. Meredith smiled at her optimism, but she couldn't explain that it went much deeper than a silly quarrel. Yet she *did* want to live at home again. She had turned down two good jobs during the week for fabricated reasons which she could now see had been a way of stalling for time. London was lonely now. It hadn't taken her many days to discover that Joss had pushed her into a form of exile and she was already rebellious.

She had to divert the conversation into a different channel and decided the time was right to broach another difficult subject.

'Speaking of quarrels,' she said, 'don't you think it's about time you made up the one with Mac Loring after all these years? I wonder you remember what it was about, and I know Mac is ready to let bygones be bygones.'

'Is he indeed!' snapped Julia, immediately bristling. But her guarded expression gradually changed into one of hesitant questioning. 'I suppose time mellows everything. Since Piers was killed I've certainly wondered about holding out an olive branch. You really think he would accept it?'

They were wandering slowly across the lawn and the conversation was punctuated with greetings from friends who were glad to see Meredith home and exclamations about the success of the barbecue. It was a strange time to be healing a feud that had lasted for a generation, yet there were reasons why it was necessary. Meredith was remembering the evening Mac had taken her out to dinner and how he had said one of his dearest wishes was to patch up the quarrel with Julia. They had talked a lot about her, and one of the things mentioned had been her project.

Meredith wiped her fingers on a paper serviette, then slipped her arm through her mother's again.

'Mummy, I'm sure you know the name of the anonymous benefactor who's so interested in your holiday centre.'

'I can guess, of course.'

'And if you're thinking it's Mac I'm sure that you're a hundred per cent right. He told me one of the things he wanted most was to put things right between you, and he knows you would never accept money, so I think this is his way of trying to make amends.' Meredith paused, giving her mother an anxious look. 'I hope you'll acknowledge it gracefully.'

Julia's face was taut with familiar suppression, but Meredith was determined it should finally be overcome and repeated her hopes until her mother's lips curved into a grin.

'Poor old Mac! I bet he feels guilty about having all that money.' She gave a mischievous laugh. 'At least some of it will be going to a very good cause. Thank goodness he acted straight away before Corinne got her greedy hands on it. If you give me his address, darling, I'll get in touch with him personally in the morning.'

Meredith gave her mother a hug, feeling as if a weight had been lifted.

'You won't regret it,' she promised. Of course there was still her father to convince, but knowing Julia's powers of persuasion she didn't think she would have to worry.

It was then that she felt a tug at her arm and when she looked down she saw the pudgy little face of Gary beaming at her. His cropped fair hair had grown and showed signs of being wavy, and he looked so happy to see her she transferred her arms from her mother to the small boy with spontaneous enthusiasm.

'Gary—I'm so pleased you're here!' she smiled.

His face was creased into an impish grin. 'We . . . me and Shaun, we wanted you to come back,' he said.

'Where is Shaun?'

It was the question she shouldn't have asked, because when she looked to where Gary pointed she found herself meeting the haughty gaze of Joss Hamblyn and her legs immediately felt as if they didn't belong to her.

He didn't look the least abashed at seeing her and there was no smile of welcome, but Shaun, whose hand he was holding, gave a yell as if he had pressed it and hurt him. He wore brown cords that somehow emphasised the length of his legs, and a green check shirt that was just right for the occasion. Of course, Joss was always right, or so he would have everyone believe.

Meredith forced a smile to her lips, then looked away, intending to draw moral support from her mother, but Julia was in demand and was already retracing her steps across the grass. So other than ignoring Joss and letting half the village see the rift between them, there was no alternative but to meet him and brazen it out. It had to be done some time anyway. She went across the path, focusing on him so that the sudden feeling of dizziness wouldn't make her unsteady.

'Hello,' she said brightly, her smile broadening in spite of the stiffness of her lips. She bent down and scooped Shaun into her arms and babbled to him inconsequentially before addressing Joss directly. 'Isn't it a wonderful evening? Where's Ellen? I haven't seen her yet. I was *so* relieved to hear the good news about Ian!'

She sounded like her mother, a sure sign that she was nervous, but she hoped it wouldn't give Joss that impression. Somehow she had to convince him he no longer mattered.

'Ellen has taken Kirsty home to bed,' he said, 'She'll be back. She was waiting for you to come.'

'But she didn't know I'd be here,' Meredith protested.

His eyes lingered on her face. '*I* knew you would.'

The supercilious assurance in his voice inflamed her. Now he, too, began to smile, obviously pleased with himself for being proved right yet again. She curbed her temper with difficulty and looked up at him, her eyes wide with innocent surprise.

'How clever of you. I came to collect the rest of my things.'

'You're enjoying being in London, then?'

'I'm loving it,' she lied.

Shaun wriggled until she set him back on his feet and he sped off across the lawn with Gary in hot pursuit.

'Funny,' said Joss, 'I had the feeling you would grow tired of it quickly and realise Edencombe has more to offer you.'

How she hated his mockery! Yet as she was about to deliver a heated reply, instinct warned her to be cautious. He was baiting her, still as prejudiced as on that dreadful day at Mac's house, but there was something in his manner that made it seem as if he wished she could convince him otherwise. She could almost believe there was a hint of appeal behind his words, but that was ridiculous.

'I love Edencombe, too,' she said softly. 'It's my home, but I can't live here. *You've* seen to that.'

She walked away from him, crying inwardly. She was afraid he might follow her and there was a pain in her chest as she hurried, but when she glanced round he was among a throng of people, only a glimpse of the green check shirt visible as he bent to talk to a child. Why was it that children liked him so much?

Her heart was thudding erratically and she didn't know which way to go. The woodsmoke stung her eyes. She was still in love with him, that was the trouble. This madness was something she couldn't control, and she couldn't possibly start each day fearful of bumping into him, so how could she even think of staying on in the village?

Some friends stopped to chat and she stood beneath the coloured lights trying to concentrate on everyday conversation, but Joss was still too near for comfort and she made an excuse to move on. A space had been cleared on the lawn and a local group had started up with a disco beat that drew the crowd and set them dancing. Meredith looked longingly towards the sanctuary of the stables, but Joss hadn't even left her that refuge, for memories of the last time she had gone there were like a barricade, and the thought of setting foot inside was electrifying.

All the same, she walked a little way down the path towards the stables, irresistibly drawn to the place where she had given herself to Joss. Away from the coloured lights there was an oasis of quiet where she could linger a minute to regain her composure, but as she stood in the shadows she became aware of stealthy movement over by the door. She watched curiously, thinking it was a young local couple in search of privacy, and when she heard giggles she felt a stab of envy. They didn't know how lucky they were to be carefree. But then as her eyes became accustomed to the gloom, she saw two small figures emerge from the shrubbery and dart inside the stables, and she realised it was Gary and Shaun up to their same old tricks.

She was about to go after them when there was a tap on her shoulder and she turned to see a young man she had known since schooldays.

'I've been looking for you,' he said. 'Everyone's dancing. Why aren't you?'

Meredith liked him. He had always made her laugh, she remembered, and what she needed was some light entertainment to revive her. She held out her hand, which he took with alacrity, and gave him a brilliant smile.

'I take it that's an invitation,' she said, and let him lead her back to the illuminated lawn where most people were now girating in time to the music.

She was popular. Partners vied with each other for a chance to dance with her and for the next half hour she succeeded in pushing Joss to the back of her mind. The last time she had seen him he had been turning sausages on the barbecue alongside her father, and she hoped that was where he would stay for the rest of the evening. She also hoped he would notice the attention she was receiving and believe he meant nothing to her, for if he knew of the comparisons she was making each time a new partner claimed her, it would be too much of a boost to his inflated ego.

No one took much notice of the smoke at first. There had been a haze of it swirling among the lights all evening, and when heavier drifts caused coughing fits it was just assumed the next batch of sausages would be browner. So the alarm was not raised until the first flame was seen licking through the stable roof, and then there was pandemonium. Not that anyone was in a panic; there was no need for it. But everyone shouted for buckets and a fire-fighting team was already under way while Howard was phoning for the fire brigade.

'Must have been a spark from the barbecue,' someone said. 'Though I can't see how it could have happened.'

Meredith had gone straight to an outhouse near the stables where old buckets had been kept for animal feed in the days when they had kept horses, and was passing them out to willing hands when she heard the comment. The roof had quickly caught hold, and she had been so concerned about preventing the fire spreading she hadn't given a thought to how it might have started.

'Oh, no!' she breathed. 'The boys are in there!'

She dashed outside and round the pond where people

were filling buckets with water. Sparks were flying now, showering down like fireworks, and she could hear the crack of burning timber. Someone was shouting for them all to move back, but the chain of people handing buckets up to two men in a tree was not broken. Meredith dipped her handkerchief in one of the buckets of water and pushed between them.

The door was open far enough for her to slip inside. Only the upper part of the stables was alight, but the whole place was filled with smoke so that it was impossible to see, and she quickly tied the wet handkerchief over her nose and mouth.

'Gary! Shaun! Are you there?' she yelled, coughing before she could repeat their names. It was possible they had left before the fire started, but somehow she was convinced they were still there, too terrified at the outcome of their mischief-making to move.

She went further in, shouting all the time, and she stumbled against something in the dense smoke. It was the ladder to the hay-loft, fallen to the ground. She picked herself up and peered upwards through the smoke until she could make out the shapes she knew instinctively would be there. Two small boys, their eyes so wide with fright they seemed to fill their faces, were lying on their stomachs on the floor above, their only way of escape cut off. If they had been calling out before, they now seemed struck dumb with fright.

'It's all right,' cried Meredith. 'I'll get the ladder back in half a minute!'

While she was struggling with it the flames curled round another rafter and kindled the dry wood immediately. The ladder was heavy and ungainly and she staggered backwards under the weight before she could balance it. She yelled to Gary, instructing him to steady the top of it as soon as it touched the beam, but not to lean forward, and minutes later both boys were